CROSS-COUNTRY LOVE

LOVE ON THE PODIUM

ERIN MCLELLAN

BLURB

Mara May is the princess of cross-country skiing. All she needs to finish her career on a high note is the gold medal she was denied four years before by firebrand, Kirby Bonham. And Kirby is still the only one standing in her way.

After upsetting the sport's princess, Kirby milks her newfound fame for all it's worth by becoming a reality-TV star. But now Kirby must prove her gold medal was more than a fluke.

Mara and Kirby have history. History of trash talk, upsets, and trading podiums. Their rivalry becomes the flashiest story in primetime when they can't keep their contempt *or* chemistry to themselves. As Mara's princess persona and Kirby's carefree façade crumble under the pressure of the Games, rivalry warps into passion. But during the most important competition of their lives, there's too much at stake to fall in love.

Cross-Country Love *is part of the Love on the Podium shared queer romance series.*

CONTENT NOTES

This novel contains descriptions of sex; explicit language; on-page panic attacks; and brief mentions of parent estrangement.

For more information, use the contact form at erinmclellan.com/contact/.

To Neva and Karen

*You deserve a gold medal for listening to my angst about writing
this book.*
I hope this dedication will do instead.

PROLOGUE

Beijing Olympics, 2022

MARA MAY KNEW the melting point of gold: 1,948 degrees Fahrenheit.

She knew the atomic mass: 196.96657 *u*.

And the atomic number: 79.

But she didn't know the weight of an Olympic gold medal around her neck. The heft of one in her palm. She didn't know how fast it might warm against her skin. Or how different a gold medal might feel versus silver and bronze.

She thought it would feel very different.

Gold.

It was Mara's sole focus. It was all that mattered.

"Mara May, have you had trouble acclimating to the altitude here in China?" a reporter from ESPN asked her.

"No. I'm fine."

It was the pre-Olympics press day, but she could hardly focus on the reporters in front of her. She was running the Beijing courses in her head. Thinking through strategies, reviewing the strengths of her competitors. Testing herself, even as she went through the motions of making nice with the media.

She was usually terrified of press conferences. She hated public speaking. Hated having eyes on her, especially without the safety of her skis. But she was too preoccupied to be nervous.

She should have been focusing on her words and not the hamster wheel in her brain. She had a reputation to uphold. A persona. To overcome her shyness, she put on a façade for the press, and even, to an extent, for her teammates.

Nicey-nice. The good girl. Polite.

But today, her heart wasn't in it. Her mind kept straying back to gold.

She wanted it. She was going to get it.

"This is a young team. How is the dynamic between the handful of veterans and all the rookies?" another reporter asked. The question was directed at her, but since he hadn't said her name, she pretended it wasn't. Eventually, someone else chimed in. Mara didn't listen to their answer.

Reporters asked questions about the wind in Zhangjiakou. The artificial snow. Covid regulations and precautions.

She let others respond. Or she gave the blandest, shortest responses. She glanced at her teammates. The closest to her was Kirby Bonham. *KB,* as everyone called her, but Mara had never felt cool enough to use the nickname. Nicknames indicated a degree of familiarity that Mara wasn't comfortable with.

Regardless, Kirby could answer. She loved to talk.

"Mara May?" said a reporter from the back row.

"Yes, sir?"

She didn't recognize the reporter's name once he gave it. None of this mattered. She smiled at him.

Gold.

She should have been resting. Or training.

"Why have you decided not to race in the relay here in Beijing?"

"I'm racing on an injury, so we're limiting impact where it makes sense to do so." She'd answered that question already, so it was annoying to answer it again.

Her hip flexor was feeling a tad weak after the Tour de Ski, so the physio had suggested dropping the less important events for the Olympics.

Not that she would ever call the relay a *less important event*. But they were an inexperienced team, and a medal was incredibly unlikely in the relay. Having extra rest in the middle of the Games was what was best for her. The relay team was not going to make the podium—with or without her—and giving up her spot provided another athlete extra experience with an Olympic start.

"The princess of cross-country skiing needs to win her gold medal," Kirby said, a slyness in her voice that made Mara bristle inside. She hated that moniker, but it had unfortunately stuck. The press used it. Her teammates used it, normally behind her back and without much kindness.

"In the thirty-k mass start?" the reporter asked. He squinted down at a card in his hand as if he were fact-checking his own question. And he probably was. Some of the reporters only cared about winter sports once the Olympics came around.

"I'm racing in the thirty kilometer, yes," Mara said. She felt too superstitious to admit that that was *the race*. That the race was hers. The gold was hers.

But it was.

Finally.

It was her third Olympics. She wasn't going to lose.

She'd won gold at the World Championships. She was the top distance skier in the world. These Olympics were her coronation, and her future was golden.

Kirby was the only other American cross-country ski racer who would match the number of kilometers Mara would put on her skis at the Olympics. For most of her career, Kirby's focus had been sprints, but in the past two years, she had started making a play for the distance races. She'd even, surprisingly, snagged the fourth start spot on the team for the thirty kilometer.

It would be good experience for Kirby to race the thirty-k. Not that Mara cared about Kirby's development as a skier.

Gold was her one and only concern.

Her only desire.

She was going to bring that gold home to Alaska.

"How does it feel racing the relay without your objectively best skier?" that same reporter asked Kirby.

Kirby lit up like the question excited her. "Mara might

be our 'best skier.'" She made air quotes with her fingers. "But she's not our fastest."

Mara didn't react. Because that was false. And because she'd trained her whole adult life, and most of her teenage life too, to lock down, tune out, and turn on the speed. The queen of compartmentalization. Or perhaps, the princess.

If she could separate herself from the intensity and pressure surrounding elite cross-country skiing, she could do the same during an irrelevant press conference.

Gold. That was all that mattered. Kirby Bonham's outrageousness did not.

"Is that so?" the reporter said.

"Fuck, yeah," Kirby said. "Mara's not our fastest skier. *I am.*"

Mara laughed. It was a small one, but it left her before she'd realized it.

All the eyes in the room landed on her, and heat rushed to her cheeks.

Kirby glanced at her and smiled. Something about that smile threw Mara's stomach for a loop. It pissed her off. And made her feel funny. Suddenly, Mara was very aware of the triphammer of her heart. Of the blood whooshing in her ears.

Kirby's smile wasn't kind. It was nasty.

And Mara wanted to see it again.

"Mara May, what's it like being rivals with your teammate?" another reporter asked. Mara recognized the reporter from the Olympics in Pyeongchang. "Is it hard to switch between being so close to your teammates, traveling together during the World Cup season, to the competitive nature of the Olympics?"

Mara wasn't close with the other skiers on the US Cross-Country Ski Team. She kept to herself, a true introvert, even as they all spent every season together and some off-seasons training in the same locations. So no. It wasn't hard.

"I don't see them as rivals," she said. "I don't see *Kirby Bonham* as a rival. I'm usually so far ahead of her, I don't see her at all."

CHAPTER
ONE

KIRBY SMACKED a carefree smile on her face and barreled into the fancy Oberhof restaurant. She was an hour late. She had on day-old mascara. And the natural deodorant she'd been gifted to film an Instagram ad wasn't quite cutting it.

But making an entrance depended on confidence, and there was no way she was ever going to let anyone on the women's US Cross-Country Ski Team see her sweat.

Smell her sweat? Maybe. See her sweat? Absolutely not.

Being late put her on the back foot. She had hoped to get the chance to settle in, to readjust. They had seven days of training and media in Oberhof, Germany before heading off to Italy for the Olympics. She was supposed to arrive the day before but had been held up in LA filming a reunion episode for a dating show. It took her a few days to transform from Kirby Bonham the reality-TV star to KB the athlete. It was mental whiplash, but at least it was whiplash of her own making.

Even if it was hard, even if it put her on lots of people's shit lists, Kirby was the architect of her own life, and she would do whatever was required to protect that.

So she walked into the private room of the restaurant like she owned it. She'd learned long ago that the only way to survive in the cross-country skiing world was to make herself so big and in your face that no one could deny her. She deserved a seat at the table, whether the table was a real one or metaphorical.

The room had moody lighting, and everyone was dressed like a fashion plate. She was greeted with cheers and a silly chant of "KB, KB, KB!"

"Ah, guys." It nearly choked her up.

Almost.

Kirby was a good time. Everyone said so. A good hang. Good TV.

She wouldn't have been able to heel-turn from skiing to reality TV and back again and again otherwise. But it was nice to be reminded that her teammates were normally happy to see her.

Most of them.

Ninety-nine percent at least.

She gave a round of hugs, even though it had only been days since she'd seen everyone at the recent World Cup event. She started with her primary coach, Coach Wu, who was wearing what Kirby could only describe as formal athleisure. Coach Wu squeezed her hard.

"How was LA?" Coach Wu asked.

It had sucked to hop from the World Cup in Europe to LA for filming and back to Europe for training and the

Olympics over a handful of days, but it was what she'd signed up for when she'd agreed to film the dating show over the summer. She'd known the reunion would film right before the Olympics. She'd figured the jet lag would be worth it.

But filming the reunion had run late, and she had missed her flight, putting her a whole day behind everyone else.

"Fine, just more drama than I expected."

"That's good, right?" Coach Wu had always been supportive of Kirby's extracurriculars, even as others gave her side-eye about it.

Kirby laughed. "Very good, yes. You get it."

Not every skier was able to make a career out of cross-country skiing for their whole lives. Not every former Olympian became coach of the Olympic team. Or a prime-time commentator. Or director of a Nordic ski association.

Kirby wasn't quite palatable enough for that shit. So she had to legacy plan in other, more creative ways.

Brandilyn Rogers and Jordan Siwa were next for hugs. They were two peas in a pod who were so fucking young and looked up to the veterans in a way that was almost uncomfortable. It was their first Olympics. Kirby was envious of their bright-eyed excitement. Everything was new and cool and special to them. Even a boring team dinner to celebrate the most stressful few weeks of their lives.

There were more hugs and jokes and rowdy hellos around the table to teammates, physios, technicians, and staff members. Most of the coaches were bunched up at the end of the table, including the head coach, Coach Redman, who barely glanced up from scribbling in his ever-present notebook to wave. He was the busiest person she had ever met.

Kirby was almost all the way around the table when she spotted *her*.

Mara May.

Her wavy, dark hair was in a high ponytail, falling halfway down her back—a back that seemed turned toward Kirby in a very deliberate way—and she had on a tight, long-sleeved periwinkle dress that somehow showed nothing and also everything.

Like those pointy-ass shoulder blades.

Ridiculous.

"Hello, Mara," Kirby said, loud enough that Mara would never be able to ignore her.

Mara turned slowly. Kirby opened her arms for a hug, which forced Mara to stand up and give her one. If Mara was anything, it was too image conscious to make a scene. She'd done that once, and it hadn't turned out well for her.

"Fancy finding you here, socializing with the peasants," Kirby said in her ear, lips brushing the soft hair that had escaped the severe ponytail.

It was unusual for Mara to attend team-building shit. She had always chosen to hold herself apart from the team.

Mara patted Kirby's back lightly twice and pulled away, all sharp angles.

"I'm not the one too busy in Hollywood to show up for training, Bonham," Mara said so quietly Kirby was sure no one else could hear.

A zip of excitement raced through Kirby. As much as she hated to admit it, she loved when Mara deigned to acknowledge her. It usually only happened on the podium.

"But I was doing something really important, you see," Kirby said, purposefully pitching her voice at a normal volume. "My ex and I had to have a public spat for money."

"How nice for you. Love is so important," Mara said, deadpan.

"You think?" As far as Kirby knew, Mara didn't do relationships. Mara didn't date other skiers at least. Because that rumor mill would have been milling.

The glare Mara gave her could have iced over a hot tub. They had known each other for practically half their lives, floating through the same orbit but never friends. Mara was one step above everyone else, but especially Kirby. Better mannered, more disciplined, more conventional.

Mara had acted like Kirby didn't exist until four years ago.

Now she would never forget.

"Where am I sitting?" Kirby asked the table, letting Mara's dirty look have the last word.

Mara turned away from her and back to the conversation she had been having with one of the only other Olympic veterans on the team, Lindsey McGrath. Lindsey blew Kirby a kiss. It would be Lindsey's second Olympic Games. She was a steady presence on the team. Unflappable. Anti-drama. Legitimately nice. She showed up, did her job, enjoyed her time, and stayed out of the spotlight.

Kirby was sure Lindsey and Mara were talking about skiing rather than something interesting, so she wasn't jealous or upset at being forced to move to the empty chair on the other side of the table beside Jordan.

Kirby chatted with Jordan, who she was rooming with in Oberhof, answering Jordan's questions about the Opening Ceremony, Olympic Village, and the crowds in Beijing and Pyeongchang. It would be Kirby's third Olympics, and she wished it felt like old hat.

But it didn't. It never stopped being overwhelming, stressful, and life-changing.

"What are you most excited about?" Kirby asked Jordan, which sent her on a chatty, adorable monologue. Kirby listened with half an ear, her gaze straying to Mara because she couldn't help it. They were around each other all the time but never in social settings. Mara was smiling so kindly at Lindsey. So different than the way she looked at Kirby. When she lowered herself enough to bother to look at Kirby.

"I know I won't medal, but I can't wait—"

"Hold up," Kirby said, interrupting Jordan. "Why do you think you won't medal?"

"Well…" Jordan kind of flailed her hands around. "We more or less know who is going to challenge in each race."

"No." Kirby stopped her again. "You don't. The relay team won a silver medal in the last Olympics, and absolutely no one believed in us before that race started. You never know who might race the best race of their life."

She didn't even mention her gold in the thirty kilometer. She was just as proud, if not prouder, of the relay silver.

Kirby glanced across the table. Mara was stock still, like she'd been frozen by a spell. Lindsey spoke, and Mara seemed to snap out of it to nod, but her posture was sharper than it had been before.

Mara had on little heart earrings that were the exact same color as her dress. Her aesthetic was… *something else.* So cutesy and playful for someone who was cold as ice. The perfect cover. The perfect mask for the princess of cross-country skiing.

She looked approachable but wasn't. Looked sweet but wasn't. And she was likely going to win one, if not two or more, gold medals in a few weeks' time.

Kirby needed to listen to her own pep talk, but it was hard not to feel like the writing was on the wall. She'd had a tough season so far, barely squeaking out some of the Olympic starting spots on her best events. And last season hadn't been much better. Setback after setback. Distraction after distraction. Training disrupted by filming. Focus disrupted by fame. She loved it and hated it.

But once the Olympics were over, what would happen to Kirby? Would she be a washed-up skier with zero outside skills? A C-list celebrity? Or something else entirely?

Kirby turned back to Jordan, but her vision was suddenly doing *that thing*. The wavy-around-the-edges thing.

Her heartbeat thumped double time, a loud clamber in her chest.

Not again.

She didn't want to have a panic attack. Not again. Not for the second time in less than a week.

They were so inconvenient. And disorienting. They

came on fast—racing heart, nausea, sweat, tingling—only to crest and dissipate as if nothing had happened.

It had been over a year since she'd had one. Maybe closer to two years. So it sucked to be staring down the barrel of two within seven days. Right before the Olympics.

She lifted her drink to her lips, but her hand was shaking so much the ice rattled. She quickly placed the glass back on the table.

Jordan chattered away, and Kirby nodded along. She needed to get a grip. She did some box breathing, trying to smile through her episode. Then star breathing. Then 4-7-8 breathing. Then she started to worry she was doing way too much breathing as her hands began to ache and cramp, symptoms the handy-dandy Internet had told her were due to a drop in carbon dioxide levels in her blood.

"I'll be right back," Kirby said and stood to go to the bathroom. She didn't want anyone to know what was going on, but it felt like she was a walking neon sign of wrongness. The attack would end soon. She just had to get through it.

The bathroom didn't have an attendant, thank God, but it did have one of those fancy seating areas. Her feet were heavy like she was postholing through deep, wet snow. She lowered herself onto a cushion, even though she hated the idea of sitting on a bathroom sofa.

It was a momentary bodily reaction. A spike of something in her brain chemistry. Something she couldn't control.

She told herself that again and again. *Just a momentary bodily reaction. It is okay to feel out of control.*

The first time this had happened, when she was fifteen, had been the same. Sudden, unexpected, and ill-timed.

It is okay to feel out of control.

She was *fine*. Everything was fine.

The bathroom door opened, so Kirby pretended to be very interested in her phone. She had texts from her best friend, Apollo, arranging breakfast with her the next day and opening the door for a booty call that night.

She tried to focus on that. To take her body's temperature. To trick it into wanting to fuck rather than going haywire in a restaurant bathroom.

A pair of adorable, pastel purple tennis shoes wavered through her peripheral vision and she almost groaned.

She didn't have to look up. It was perfectly acceptable to just ignore—

Who was she kidding? Mara May was hard to ignore.

Mara's steps stuttered as she met Kirby's eyes. Kirby's jaw hurt.

"Are you okay, Bonham?" Mara asked, unsmiling and serious as always.

"Yeah. Are you?" Kirby's voice was needlessly snappy, but she didn't have control over herself at all.

Mara's head tipped to the side, and she scowled. "I'm not the one hiding in the bathroom."

"I'm not hiding," Kirby said, but Mara had already moved from the seating area to the sinks. She stopped at a mirror to fix her flawless hair and put on shiny pink lipgloss.

Kirby stood up abruptly. The world shimmered around her, but she ignored it. There was nothing to hide.

CHAPTER
TWO

NINE DAYS until the Opening Ceremony.

Ten to skiathlon.

Twenty-five to the inaugural Olympic women's fifty-kilometer mass start.

Mara had so many countdowns in her head, there wasn't space left for much else, but on the third day of training in Oberhof, the cameras arrived. They brought with them even more mental disruptions. She had expected it, but she didn't like it. They had been given the team filming schedule at dinner, and that morning they were shuffled into the room with the best light at the training center to film some B-roll.

Everyone seemed so comfortable, but she couldn't loosen up. She sat among her teammates, stiff as a board. Memories of last time, of the press conference before Beijing, rushed at her. She'd acted so out of character and had regretted it.

"Mara, did they have dial-up Internet in the Olympic Village during your first Olympics?" Jordan Siwa asked.

"Very cute." Mara smiled at her young teammate. She certainly felt old, and comments about her long career were nothing new. They just usually didn't happen in front of television cameras and boom mics and portable lighting.

But if there had been no cameras, her teammates wouldn't have joked with her at all. She wasn't exactly a leader to impressionable young athletes, even if that was the story the powers-that-be were hoping to push.

Mara struggled balancing her own needs and the team spirit that was expected during the Olympics. And she'd had enough Olympic experience to know. She required extra rest, zen, and alone time during competition. *"Not a team player"* a coach in Alaska had said once when she'd been a teenager. Mara's father had promptly removed her from that club and trained her himself.

Because Coach Dad had historically worked out so well for so many athletes.

She wasn't exactly beloved by the other men and women on the US Cross-Country Ski Team and never had been. But her objective was to win, not to girl talk with a bunch of kids getting their first taste of the Olympic rings.

Unfortunately, the cameras *were* there. They *were* being filmed, and she had to play her role. She wasn't going to mess it up like last time.

She was the story. Half of it, at least.

"She's not quite that old," another rookie, Brandilyn, said, playfully snapping a USA-branded towel. "I bet she commemorated it on MySpace, though."

Mara nodded and tried to shape her face into something sweet and acceptable. She had to play along even though playing along, joking along, hell, just getting along wasn't quite her thing.

"Yes, sure. Because I had so much time for MySpace back in the olden days." Not exactly a sparkling joke, but Mara hoped it passed well enough.

She'd had multiple meetings with her agent, the US Ski and Snowboard communications team, and the Cross-Country Ski Team press officer.

Their goal… No, *her* goal was to solidify her legacy—on the course and off. If that meant playing the princess, she would play the princess. If it meant controlling herself, she would control herself. She'd learned her lesson four years ago. She was following a script this time—smiling big, saying nothing.

"Was it hard for you to find eight friends, Mara May? Seems like it might be." That voice—warm and smoky—was like ice water on top of Mara's mood. She tried not to glance at Kirby Bonham.

Tried and failed.

You never knew which Kirby might show up on any given day.

Resourceful, dynamic, talented.

Messy, dramatic, attention-seeking.

It was a crapshoot, and Mara hated the unknown.

Today, Kirby had on all black workout clothes. Last night, she had been wearing black too. A black tank top, a distressed black leather jacket, black chunky boots, jeans that seemed to have been made for her alone. She always looked so striking and so *herself*. She was a brand, after all.

Kirby had more media exposure than everyone in the room combined.

Good exposure. Bad exposure. It didn't matter. Kirby was just as likely to hock a meal kit on Instagram as she was to appear on reality TV.

Mara swallowed hard. *Remember the cameras. Remember the cameras.* "Only someone our age would understand that reference, Bonham."

She would bet her favorite sunglasses that most of the skiers around her had no idea what a MySpace page looked like, much less the drama surrounding who was in your "top eight."

"Are you two not friends, KB?" the television producer asked, directing the question to Kirby. He had been silent up to that point, just trying to get "some color," he'd said, by filming the team horsing around before they left for Italy.

Everyone in the room went silent.

No. They were not friends.

"I'm friendly," Kirby said, her smile sharky. *That smile.* It did things to Mara's stomach. Made her feel nervous, uncomfortable, and frustrated all at once. "Right, Mara May?"

"Of course. You're a ray of sunshine, Bonham." Mara despised how Kirby said her name. All sing-songy like it was a joke.

"Yep. *Golden.* That's me."

Heat flushed over Mara's face as those words sunk in.

Mara opened her mouth, suddenly worked up in a way that only Kirby elicited. Kirby got under Mara's skin, and she had no idea why.

Mara couldn't afford to lose control this time.

She was the "good girl." There were expectations, false as they were. A good leader. A good person. *Nice, nice, nice.* But that little word—*golden*—threatened to bring it all down.

Before Mara ruined her carefully crafted persona, a loud thunderclap sounded from the far side of the room, and all of them snapped to attention.

Mara's main coach, Ulf Karlsson, was standing by Coach Stacy Wu in the doorway, out of the camera's view. They were foils to each other. Coach Karlsson was stoic and blunt. Coach Wu was funny and kind.

But it was Coach Wu who had clapped. When she wanted to, she had the ability to bring every single one of them back to their childhood selves. Frankly, some of her teammates weren't that far removed from the Junior Nordic Ski Team.

"That's enough of this." Coach Wu waved her immaculately manicured fingertips toward the camera crew in dismissal. "More tomorrow. It's time to ski. Skate skis today."

As they got their gear on, Mara put her head down and worked to calm herself. She hated that one word from Kirby had the ability to crack her.

Mara wanted to will everyone away. She didn't like team training sessions. It was awkward. Everyone was so nice and supportive, and she didn't have that good teammate mode dialed in, even after all these years.

Her mom called her shy. Her dad said she was focused.

She was pretty sure lots and lots of people said she was a bitch. She tried not to worry about that, but she felt very *observed* this time around. Everyone expected her to win a gold medal, or several. Everyone was watching to see if she choked again.

Ten days until her first event.

Twenty-five until her last.

A staff member opened the locker room door. "KB? Mara? Some dude from US Ski and Snowboard wants to talk to you both in the hall. Together."

Mara's eyes immediately went to Kirby. She was almost completely geared up. And as much as Mara felt like she and Kirby were diametrically opposed on all things, she could see her own unease mirrored in Kirby.

"That sounds ominous," Kirby joked. "Do you know what this is about?"

"No." Mara just wanted to race. She wanted to train, preferably by herself, and race, and win. She didn't want to have meetings, or be filmed, or have to spend a second longer than necessary with Kirby Bonham.

———

An older man gave Kirby a sour look as she approached him in the hallway. She'd met him before. Lots of times, but she was terrible at remembering the names of self-important men. Larry, maybe? Barry?

He'd once told her she should stop cursing in her online videos, and she'd promptly disregarded him for all eternity.

"A word, Miss Bonham?" Blarry said.

"Okay." Kirby steeled herself.

"You as well, Miss May, if it's not too much trouble?" he said.

Gosh, how courteous.

"What's this about?" Kirby asked as Blarry escorted them away from the locker room and into an empty office.

He ignored Kirby, only looking at Mara. "I'm so sorry to interrupt your training, ladies, but I'd like to chat."

"That's quite all right," Mara said politely. Such a teacher's pet.

"I'll make this brief. It's been made clear to us that the television networks intend to make your history a large storyline during the Olympics. We've been contacted by producers and journalists," he said. "But we do not agree with the rivalry approach. We would prefer to have a united front."

Who was *we*? Because fostering a rivalry worked quite well for Kirby.

Mara trash talking Kirby four years ago was honestly one of the best things that had ever happened to her. It had catapulted her into the public consciousness and pushed her to prove Mara wrong.

Kirby skied better mad. Milking their rivalry for attention had zero downsides as far as she was concerned.

Blarry droned on. "We don't think pushing the conflict angle is the right thing for you."

"You mean it's not the right thing for Mara," Kirby said.

He didn't contradict that. "Or our sport. The Olympic Games are our chance to reach a wider American audience and bring new people in."

And new money, but Kirby knew better than to say that.

He continued, "It's a ground-level opportunity to get kids and their families interested in cross-country skiing, and they'll be our Olympians of the future."

Gag.

That sounded nice but was just a bunch of marketing bullshit.

"Cross-country skiing is not as appealing if the primary narrative surrounding the sport is catty and ugly," Blarry finished.

Rivalries in men's sports were never described as catty. Cross-country skiing had instituted equal racing distances for men and women for the Milan Cortina Olympics, but that equality didn't always extend to how men and women were treated as athletes and people.

"We don't create an ugly atmosphere," Mara said. "We hardly speak to each other."

"You hardly speak to anyone," Kirby said before she could stop herself.

"Quips like that are precisely what I'm talking about, Miss Bonham," Blarry said. "Another example is your disruptive dig at Mara in the locker room during what would have otherwise been a nice team segment."

Mara wrinkled her nose but didn't say anything. It was annoying that he was sniveling all over Mara as if she were actually a princess. Mara had held her own in that locker room. She was fine.

"I'm sorry. I'm terrible. What's your name again?" Kirby asked.

"Chandler Wendleton," he bit out.

Whoops. So not Larry or Barry.

"He's the head of public relations for US Ski and Snowboard," Mara said. Little know-it-all.

"So what exactly are you asking us to do, Chandler?" Kirby said. She was over this. At this rate, she and Mara would be kilometers behind the rest of the team, and Kirby loved skiing with the team.

"You're being tapped for a pre-filmed, joint interview with Janette Collins."

"Seriously?" Kirby said loudly. "Fuck."

Mara looked shocked. And maybe a little sick too.

Holy shit, that was a big draw. It was the type of interview that could get Kirby her next sponsorship or gig on a show. Janette Collins's interviews were a staple of Olympic primetime coverage.

"I'm sure you've both got voicemails from your agents. The network and Ms. Collins's team were kind enough to loop us in as well. We cannot control you. But I am asking you to keep the animosity low. Tell interviewers you're *friends* and teammates who support each other."

"You want us to lie?" Kirby said.

"I want you to bury the hatchet. Or if that's beyond you, pretend to. Let the narrative be the transformative nature of forgiveness and friendship."

Kirby laughed. "Forgiveness? And what are we supposed to be forgiving each other for? Spicy interviews? Am I supposed to ask forgiveness for winning Mara's gold medal?" She turned to Mara. "Do you have anything to say about this?"

Mara shrugged. "It's easy to say we're friends if asked. I don't feel the need to make headlines."

Kirby rolled her eyes so hard it almost gave her vertigo. Making headlines led to making money in her experience. Yes, she loved skiing. She was good at it. But skiing alone didn't pay the bills.

"Don't you think a rivalry also makes people invested in our sport? That's why she wants to talk to us. Because of what happened in Beijing. Viewers will see we're competitive. And that winning matters to us. It makes our races against each other exciting for viewers. Gives them someone to root for and root against."

"Do you want to be the one who's rooted against?" Chandler Wendleton said bluntly. "Forgive me, Miss Bonham, but you can be polarizing."

And Mara was not. It went unsaid. Mara had made one snide comment about Kirby four years ago but had kept her mouth shut since. She was undeniably the face of American cross-country skiing to anyone who actually paid attention to it.

And everyone who actually paid attention to cross-country skiing also thought Kirby had allowed herself to be distracted by lowbrow television endeavors for four years.

"We would prefer if the focus was on rooting against other countries," Chandler continued. "Rather than beating each other."

That was ridiculous. They *were* competitors. In the one event they raced together, one of them would place higher than the other. That fact didn't change because they were both competing under the American flag.

"We'll be nice," Mara said. "Or I will be. Kirby can make the choices that are best for her career." Mara very deliberately tugged her gloves on. "I'd like to start skiing now."

"Very well. Thank you for your time, ladies." Chandler gave Mara one last smile before spinning on his heels and leaving without a glance in Kirby's direction.

She was used to that. Used to being dismissed. But she was also good at making people regret it.

CHAPTER
THREE

MARA AND KIRBY hit the course at the same time. Coach Karlsson waved them on and told them how far behind the rest of the team they were.

Mara wanted to vomit.

That meeting had been bad enough. Finding out about an interview with Janette Collins was even worse. And now Mara had to ski with Kirby. And no one else. It was like her worst nightmares had collided.

She poled hard to drop Kirby, hoping she would get the hint.

She didn't.

"Okay, bestie, what did you think of all that nonsense?" Kirby asked, catching Mara and matching her tempo.

Mara wasn't used to chatting while she skied. She didn't intend to start now. She pushed ahead again, going faster than they were supposed to for a warm-up.

Kirby didn't let that stop her. She put in a burst of speed

to catch up. "No, seriously. What's your plan with that interview and feature about us?"

"What do you mean?"

The Olympics were entertainment for the television networks. They wanted to make money, and one of the ways to do that was highlighting human interest stories. To tell the viewing public, most of whom didn't care at all about winter sports, about the athletes who sacrificed so much to do what they loved. It was what Mara had adored about the Olympics as a child, watching them like a soap opera on TV.

But those stories weren't all real. They were crafted and condensed and packaged for entertainment value.

Her story, her life—*their* lives—would be packaged for entertainment value.

"We don't have to do what old Chandler Wendleton says. *We* could have a plan. We could be on the same page. Don't you think?" Kirby shrugged like that would be so easy.

But nothing was easy for Mara. Every interview, every video, every team interaction—they were hard. Always had been. And Kirby just made them harder.

Kirby had made the dig at Mara about not having friends as soon as the cameras were rolling in the locker room like it was a *Real Housewives* reunion. Her insult hadn't been about racing. It wasn't normal trash talk. Mara didn't have experience in front of cameras like Kirby. She didn't literally create drama for money.

There was no way they would ever be on the same page.

There would never be equal footing when it came to their media acumen.

When Mara didn't answer fast enough, Kirby said, "It can be for both our benefits. We don't have to tell the story they want us to tell. We're really going to pretend to be best buddies? I mean, surely you don't like this any more than I do. Four years ago, you—"

"You have no idea what story I want to tell, Bonham," Mara said quickly. She didn't want to talk about four years ago.

She glanced at Kirby and caught her jaw ticking. Mara snapped her gaze away and focused on the snowy trail.

"Fine. But we can help each other here. It doesn't have to be combative."

"*I'm* not combative." Mara stabbed her poles into the snow with way more force than necessary.

There was no love lost between her and Kirby. They did not mesh as people. Oil and water.

And now that the Olympics had come back around, that tension was a spectacle.

But a spectacle did not help Mara. It did nothing but hurt her. She refused to fall into Kirby's trap again. That had worked four years ago. It wouldn't happen this time.

Kirby sighed, and for the first time Mara could remember, she sounded tired. "I thought it would be easier to work as teammates on these interviews. *For real*. No surprises. What do *you* want the narrative to be? Until just now, no one had said a word to me about media strategy, so I'm not exactly compelled to follow their lead."

Had US Ski and Snowboard not discussed *anything* with

Kirby? Mara and her agent had had meetings on meetings for months. They'd been pushing media training at her too.

"I'm going to tell the truth," Mara said.

"And what's the truth to you, Mara May? Because I doubt your truth is mine. What will you say when Janette Collins asks about what happened in Beijing?"

"You won. What else is there to say?"

"Don't bullshit me. You gotta give me something. If you want the story to be about your triumphant final Olympics, that's fine."

"I've never said it will be my last Olympics."

"Oh, for fuck's sake. Okay, Mara. I won't mention dreaded *retirement* if it's too *spoooooky* for you."

That almost made Mara laugh. Damn Kirby's charisma.

"How about we do a little sprinkle of the narrative you want—redemption or legacy or whatever—and a teaspoon of what I want?" Kirby said. "Voilà. Magic."

Mara could not even imagine what story Kirby wanted to push. She was sure she would hate it.

They passed through a cluster of trees and hit a clearing. The rest of the team had come into sight, which meant Mara and Kirby were skiing faster than they should have been for low-intensity training. It was impressive considering they'd been talking the whole time.

There was nothing low intensity about how Mara was feeling right then.

"I don't like being told what to do. What to say," Kirby said, filling Mara's deliberate silence. "I don't play nice just because someone told me to."

That was all well and good, except Mara would be on the receiving end.

"What a shock," Mara said under her breath. She tried to focus on her pole placement, weight transfer, and glide. She treated every training session, every run, every workout as a building block meant to better her technique and conditioning. That was hard to do with Kirby's annoying voice in her ear. She wanted this conversation to be over. "As far as I'm concerned, neutrality is key. I'll say we're friends because that's the path of least resistance, and that's easier than saying you—and everyone else—are nothing but a bib number to me when thinking about the calculus of a race. You barely ping my radar."

They spent so much of their lives together, in competition and on a team, and Mara always acted as if Kirby barely existed. Because it was an easy, underhanded way to hurt her.

And it did seem to hurt her. Kirby looked ready to scream.

"You are so sweet and agreeable around everyone else," Kirby said, her voice slippery and scary soft. "It's so interesting to see what comes up now that we're alone and no one is around to see what's really inside you."

A weird shimmer of awareness flickered at the base of Mara's spine, and *lower*. She pushed the sensation to the back of her mind and locked it away.

"You are so frustrating," she said, panting from the effort of staying slightly in front of Kirby.

Nine days to the Opening Ceremony. Ten to skiathlon. Fifteen to the freestyle ten kilometer. Twenty-five to the fifty kilometer. And after that, all eyes would be off her. She could finish out the World Cup season on a high. And never have to think about Kirby again. *Heaven.*

"So no compromise, then?" Kirby continued in that poisonous voice. "Do you want me to tell Janette Collins that you overestimated yourself. Underestimated everyone else. You were too good to be on the relay, but we won silver without you. You had some of your worst showings ever on your other races. You—"

"None of that matters anymore." God, how false that was. It consumed Mara. It was all she could think about when she laid in bed at night. Every terrible millisecond of the Beijing Olympics. All her regrets. "I spent the past four years proving I am more than a few bad races. You spent the past four years proving you know how to make good TV."

Kirby laughed.

Mara had heard Kirby laugh a million times. She laughed so easily, like it was such a simple thing. She had one of those laughs that was contagious and effortless and quick.

But Mara had never heard Kirby laugh like *this*. Dark and sharp.

Mara almost stopped in her tracks just to map the sound.

"God, I don't know why I love it so much when you're bitchy," Kirby said, starting to breathe harder from exertion.

Mara's body suddenly felt like a pinball machine, pinging all over the place in warning.

They had nearly reached their cluster of teammates.

Coach Wu was at the back of the pack, and she slowed down to wait for them.

"I intend to do what's been asked of me," Mara said. The end. She was done.

"Slow it down, ladies. That's not low tempo," Coach Wu said mildly. "You're all caught up."

Mara nodded. "Yeah. Sorry, Coach."

Coach Wu patted her shoulder as Mara skied by.

She heard Coach Wu say, "You okay, KB?"

She heard Kirby say, "Not really, no."

But Mara didn't stop. Kirby Bonham wasn't her business. And she wasn't Kirby's.

JANETTE COLLINS LOOKED AIRBRUSHED. Her skin was perfection. No pores or blemishes even under the harsh lights. It was impressive.

"Once this interview is over, I'm going to have to ask for your skin care routine," Kirby said, making small talk as they waited for Mara to arrive. "I'll take notes."

"Oh, his name is Dr. Tejura. He regrows me a new face every few months."

Kirby grinned. "I love a miracle worker. Usually celebrities say, 'Oh, I don't have a routine, I just use SPF.'"

Janette laughed, and it was such a friendly, infectious laugh that Kirby's shields immediately went up. It would be so easy to let her guard down around the journalist.

Kirby got more comfortable in her chair, trying to project confidence she didn't really feel.

Mara walked in and froze when she saw them. Her hair was down, which was unusual, and Kirby stared at her for too long. Mara was a beautiful woman. She could have been as disarming as Janette if she would lose the stick up her ass.

They got Mara set up in the chair beside Kirby. She smelled fancy, and it kind of pissed Kirby off.

The cameras started to roll, and they were on.

"Mara, let's begin with simple shop talk," Janette said.

Because of course they would start with Mara.

"Okay," Mara said.

"For your entire career, you have competed in almost all Olympic cross-country ski events and disciplines. You've done freestyle and classic. You've done sprints and distance races. But there are whispers that that will not be the case this time."

Mara looked at Janette blankly.

Kirby got antsy after too many seconds of silence and jumped in. "That's hardly a rumor. Mara didn't compete in the sprint events at the last World Championships."

"Your events," Janette said.

Kirby shrugged. "I plan to compete in four events, a mix of sprint and distance races." She did better without huge breaks between starts, so racing in as many events as possible was the optimal strategy for her. "I'm not just a sprinter anymore. I proved that four years ago."

Kirby deserved to be in that fifty-kilometer race and the other events too. It irritated her that everyone treated the distance races like Mara May's preordained due.

The press, US Ski and Snowboard, their teammates—they'd all done the same thing four years ago. They'd acted like that gold was already on Mara's neck, and everyone else was table dressing at her coronation. And they'd all been wrong.

Mara let out an inaudible sigh but didn't respond to Kirby's needling.

Mara was so uptight in interviews. It was hard to play off her, to get a natural rapport going.

"Then is it true?" Janette asked Mara. "You're not planning to do any sprint events."

"It's true."

"What's your reasoning?" Janette said, seemingly unfazed by Mara's bland answer.

Kirby wasn't unfazed. She wanted the spicy Mara. The Mara with bite. She wanted Mara to reveal her true self, to level the playing field.

Janette continued, "You are currently the sport's preeminent and most well-rounded competitor. It's amazing that you have managed to dominate in so many events for so long. Why have you made the change?"

Kirby couldn't keep her scoff in, and Mara glanced at her. She looked like she was grinding glass with her teeth.

"I've gotten older," Mara said. "I've juggled knee and hip flexor injuries off and on in recent years."

"That's true but not the truth," Kirby said, infusing her voice with as much fake sweetness as possible. She didn't understand what it was about Mara that made her feel so mean, but she suddenly resented this whole circus.

If the purpose was to set up Mara as cross-country royalty, Kirby wasn't playing along.

"And what do you think the truth is, Bonham?" Mara

asked blandly, and Kirby resisted the urge to fist pump. Getting Mara to acknowledge her at all was a win.

"You want your gold medal."

"Of course."

"So you're putting your energy into the events where you have the best chance of medaling. Quality versus quantity. It's a common tactic. It doesn't make you special. It just makes you strategic."

Mara didn't respond. She went back to clenching her jaw and blankly staring at Janette.

"What do you have to say to that?" Janette asked, her voice soft and conciliatory, like she was trying to coax Mara out of her shell. It wasn't going to work. Mara's shell was made of steel.

"Nothing."

Kirby almost laughed. Mara's blandness was impressive.

"Maybe your motivation is something else. Redemption, perhaps?" Janette said.

The temperature in the room plummeted. Mara had already been all sharp angles and discomfort. Now with the roundabout reference to her losses in Beijing, she was even icier.

"Part of competing is learning from and letting go of your losses and mistakes. Focusing on the next race. Otherwise, it would be torture."

It was a rote answer, straight out of a media training handbook, but Kirby couldn't help but wonder if it was true.

She certainly hadn't let go of her win against Mara. She

held tight to it, treasured it as proof she was worthy. Sometimes she took it back out when the world tried to batter her down, to tell her she didn't deserve to be there.

"This is the first Olympic Games where men and women are racing equal distances," Janette said. "You'll both be racing in the very first Olympic women's fifty-kilometer mass start. Four years ago, your longest race was thirty kilometers. What do you think of these changes?"

"It's about time," Kirby said. "There should never have been a question that women are just as capable as men at longer distances. Other sports don't have different distances for women and men. Swimming doesn't. Track and field doesn't. Why should cross-country skiing?"

Kirby believed that with her whole heart, but it was no secret she had struggled with the fifty-k. Coming up in the sport as a sprinter, she'd had a hard time adjusting. She always finished it, and sometimes she raced it well, but not like Mara. Almost doubling the distance had been a cake walk for Mara. It had made her even more dominant. She probably would have loved to add another twenty kilometers.

"Mara, what would it mean to you to be the first ever winner of the women's fifty kilometer in the Olympics?"

And of course, Mara got that question. Not Kirby. Because Kirby wasn't expected to the be the first ever.

Upset of the century, every sports page had said four years ago. No one anticipated a repeat.

"Umm." Mara scanned the back of the room like she was trying to find an answer. But all that was back there were faces they couldn't see because the lights were shining so brightly. Her gaze wandered until it landed on Kirby. "It would be great, but I haven't really thought about it. Winning the race is important to me but not because I'd be the first to ever do it."

"Oh, I call bullsh—bull on that," Kirby said before she could stop herself. "Mara, think of the Wikipedia entries!"

Mara shot daggers at her with her eyes. Kirby loved it.

"There's a gravity around the race," Mara conceded. "It feels big and important, but my goal is to do my best. It's all I can control. Do you care about it, Bonham? Being the first to win gold in the fifty?"

"Aww, thank you for asking," Kirby said sweetly, since she wasn't getting the question from Janette Collins. "First times can be so special, can't they? But ultimately, they're rarely the most important. It would be cool to win it but not because I'd be the first women's fifty-kilometer gold medalist."

"Why then?" Janette asked.

"Because it would prove everyone wrong about me." Kirby met Mara's eyes. "And nothing gets me going more than that."

Mara twitched like she'd been zapped. Like the *real* Mara, the one she occasionally showed Kirby, was trying to escape.

"Have you always felt like you have something to prove?" Janette asked.

"I didn't come up in this sport the way other athletes do. I've had to fight to belong, to have support, to continue to afford to ski."

"I've heard you talk about your history with skiing and

how you started. It's a bit uncommon, correct?" Janette said.

"I was plucked out of a recreational, after-school skiing club when Coach Wu saw me at an event and thought I had potential. She took me under her wing and helped develop me as an athlete. I didn't even own my own skis or boots."

"And this unconventional start made you feel like you didn't belong?"

"I'm queer, so there's been a fight in my own life, in my own family, outside of skiing, to belong. I deserve to take up space. In life and in our sport. But cross-country skiing can be cliquey. It's insular."

"Do you feel accepted now? You're an Olympic gold medalist."

"It depends." Kirby tried to borrow some of Mara's steel spine. "I love my teammates. I'm close to most of them. Apollo James's family has practically adopted me since I started training in Vermont. I spend holidays with them. It's not usually athletes or coaches who make me feel *less than*. Sometimes it is but not usually."

"Well, on that note, I've heard rumors you two are close despite your past issues," Janette said. "You've taken potshots at each other through the years, most notably right before the Beijing Olympics, but pictures of you training together came out just yesterday. So how is your relationship now?"

"We're teammates," Kirby said.

"Are you friends?" Janette asked. She'd so clearly been fed this line of questioning. It felt incredibly contrived.

"Yes," Mara said at the same time Kirby said, "No."

A long silence followed their answers.

Mara looked green, her eyes wide.

"Would either of you like to expand on that?" Janette asked.

"No," Mara said quickly.

Kirby took a deep breath. She could tell the truth, or she could fake it.

She could burn it down.

Or she could play nice like she'd been asked.

She'd built her life brick by brick. She'd had helpers along the way, but she was the main architect. And she was going to be the only one to burn it down too.

"Let me just say, it was made clear to me recently that I was expected to say Mara and I are good friends," Kirby said. "Which was news to me."

MARA TURNED to Kirby with murder in her veins. Janette seemed equally surprised.

Comparison was supposedly the thief of joy, but Mara had learned early on that her job was to measure up to her competition. Judge them. Analyze. Evaluate. And win.

By her analysis, there were two objectively gorgeous, dynamic women sitting in front of her, ready to take her down in whatever arena possible. It wasn't a fair fight.

And Kirby made Mara want to brawl.

Or run away.

Fight or flight.

She couldn't do either during the interview, though. Instead, she'd planned to keep her conscience and hands clean, unlike last time in Beijing.

To freeze. And lie.

But Kirby had blown that plan to smithereens.

"It sounds as if someone asked you to play nice for this interview," Janette said. "Was it Mara?"

"No!" Mara said.

"Of course not. Mara would never," Kirby said with a laugh.

"Well, then who?"

"It wasn't Coach Wu or any other ski team staff. People can connect the dots from there, but that's all I'll say."

"We were simply asked to be professional," Mara ground out.

"Potato, potahto."

Mara had suspected Kirby might not play along, but she hadn't expected her to make it seem like a whole ridiculous and underhanded scheme.

"Well, since we're not hiding that you have bad blood, let's get to the elephant in the room," Janette said. "Four years ago, during the cross-country skiing press conference before the Olympics, Mara, you said something very out of character about Kirby. My team and I went back and scoured the Internet. We never found another interview quite like that one. What happened?

Mara had known this was coming. And she'd thought it through. She'd practiced. Thank God, because her mind was spinning. "I regret that. The Olympics are a pressure cooker. There's a lot of intensity. We're competitive, and we all care a lot. I shouldn't have said what I said. I crossed a line."

Her voice sounded thin and rushed, but she held it together.

"What? No," Kirby said. "I loved it."

Mara bit the inside of her cheek and tried not to outwardly react.

"Really?" Janette said. "It wasn't very sportsmanlike."

"So?" Kirby said. "It got so many more eyes on our race. I like the attention. And it put this enormous chip on my shoulder. Which worked out well for me."

"Okay, let's talk about *that* race. The thirty-kilometer mass start. The one that changed everything for both of you," Janette said. "One of the headlines about Mara after the Beijing Olympics was 'always a bridesmaid, never a bride,'" Janette said, directing her calculating gaze to Mara. "How would you describe your history of silver and bronze Olympic medals, Mara?"

There was an awkward silence as Mara tried to figure out how to respond. She didn't thrive under the spotlight like some people.

"I'm proud of my silver and bronze medals. I—"

"Wait," Kirby interrupted. Enter *some people*. Kirby had been stepping all over her answers from the beginning of the interview, and Mara was tired of it. "Am I the bride to Mara's bridesmaid in this scenario? I like that," Kirby continued. "A bride. Better than what I'm usually called."

"And what's that?" Janette said.

"A thief. I robbed the sport's precious star of *her* gold medal in her best event. Snatched it right out of her hands at the finish line."

Mara sent Kirby another *what-the-fuck* look. "You didn't steal anything. I lost gas at the end. You made the right move at the right time to beat me. That's part of competing."

That was what Mara was supposed to say. And on the surface, it was the truth.

Almost the truth.

Mara had thought she'd had the gold in the bag until the very end. She'd slowed down because she'd been gassed, yes, but also because she never expected Kirby to be able to challenge her on the final climb and straightaway. When she'd realized it was Kirby who she was drafting with, she'd immediately thought, *If it's just us at the end, I'm a gold medalist.* They'd come into the stadium together, and Mara had already been celebrating in her head. She'd expected Kirby to drop off. Anticipated it. She'd been unable to readjust when it didn't happen. It had been a photo finish. She'd gotten silver. And it had absolutely been her fault.

That *had* been Mara's medal to win. Olympic gold was all she was missing.

And if she didn't get gold this time... Mara didn't want to let her mind go there.

"Mara's too nice. I wouldn't be that nice if I were in her place."

"What would you say in her place?" asked Janette.

"'The twenty-fifth best skier won that day.' I hadn't even qualified for that event until I earned the discretionary spot during training the week before. I wasn't expected to hit the top twenty, much less the podium. I knew I could, but no one else believed in me. She wasn't worried about me. She had to have been thinking about Svea Solberg—"

"From Sweden," Janette clarified. Someone had done their homework.

Kirby nodded. "Who is one of the strongest finishers our sport has ever seen, or Lakyn Lopez from Canada who had won the World Cup Crystal Globe for distance races the year before."

Never mind that Mara had won every distance Crystal Globe since. Mara had also hit the podium for every fifty-k she'd raced since the new distance had been implemented. But she couldn't unclench her teeth fast enough to get the words out.

She started going through her checklist to calm down.

Seven days to the Opening Ceremony.

Eight until her first event, the skiathlon, where she would race twenty kilometers, ten in classic style and ten in freestyle. Twenty-three days until the fifty kilometer and the end of her Olympic career.

"She wasn't worried about little Kirby Bonham from Bumfu—Bumfiddle, Minnesota," Kirby said.

Mara's brain felt fuzzy. "That's not true."

It was *so* true. Mara hadn't given Kirby a second thought before that race. She'd literally said so during the press conference. She'd said she didn't *see* Kirby Bonham. Kirby didn't matter to her in the least. She hadn't paid attention to her teammates' successes or failures as long as they didn't affect her.

Well, Kirby's success had certainly affected Mara.

"Mara knows to watch for me now. I've beaten her more than once since then."

Mara's face distorted into something ugly against her will. The interview had gone so off the rails. She struggled with interviews under peak conditions. How the hell was she supposed to make it through an interview unscathed when she was getting pressed by Janette Collins and provoked by Kirby Bonham.

She wasn't supposed to make it through this. That was Kirby's goal.

"Three times. You've beaten me three times. And you haven't won a race, *any race*, against me in two years."

Not the best comeback, but it felt so satisfying to say exactly what she was thinking. A wild whip of adrenaline shot through her.

Mara wasn't looking at the camera or Janette. And neither was Kirby. They were staring at each other instead. Kirby was flushed and her eyes were a striking, bright blue.

"Underestimate me again, Mara," Kirby said, her voice dangerously soft.

Mara had had it. She'd spent four years trying to be polite and bland and boring. But she was also competitive. And everything in her rebelled at losing to Kirby, even if the only thing she was losing was a verbal sparring match.

"Or what? You'll trash me in a confessional on *Celebrity Temptation Paradise Hotel* or whatever it's called. You'll make a mean video about me on TikTok? I'm not scared of you."

The shocked silence should have made Mara snap out of it, but instead, it made her feel like she was soaring. It felt *amazing* to fight with Kirby. To finally take out some carefully controlled anger on her. To see *that* smile from Kirby again, the one that had rolled her four years ago in that godforsaken press conference.

Because saying what she'd said four years ago had felt amazing too. Until it hadn't.

"Oh *meow*. I love when you prove you actually have a personality, Mara."

"You peaked in Beijing. I'm still climbing."

Kirby was breathing fast. Mara was too.

A lock of Kirby's short, wavy hair was stuck to the side of her neck. Her throat was glistening with sweat. Mara's mind whited out, and her heartbeat exploded in her chest. She was sure she'd turned red. It felt like anger, but it was more complicated than that. Anger mixed with something messy and pulse-pounding that Mara wasn't willing to name.

"Speaking of reality TV," Janette said, and both Mara and Kirby jumped. Mara had forgotten Janette was there. "What do your teammates think about your turns in the television spotlight, KB?"

Kirby was still staring at Mara when she answered. "Ask them. Not me. I like being on TV. I like making money."

"Fair enough," Janette said. "Mara, what do you think about Kirby doing competition reality shows?"

"I've done two dating shows as well," Kirby said, and for some reason, that made Mara even angrier. "Neither one is *Celebrity Temptation Paradise Hotel*, but I'd go on that show too if it existed."

"Bonham can do what she wants with her free time."

"Oh, should I translate that for you too, Janette?" Kirby asked.

"By all means." Janette gestured and smiled.

Kirby changed her posture, sat up straighter, and primly put her hands in her lap. Kirby was impersonating her. She pretended to flip her hair over her shoulder. *"Bonham* can waste her time making more money than she ever has skiing by selling her soul to trash TV, but the rest of us have to keep our hearts pure and our hands clean for *athletics."*

That impression hurt. It hurt like Mara was fourteen years old and being snubbed at the lunch table, which was ridiculous. She was thirty-four. Plus, she probably deserved to be called stuck up. But a dig at that aspect of her personality pressed on a childhood bruise that had never healed.

"So your stints on TV are about the money?" Janette asked Kirby.

"A girl's gotta eat."

It wasn't about the money. Or not *just* about the money. Kirby was a spotlight hog. She was hungry for attention. She'd milked the aftermath of her surprise gold medal with a voraciousness that would have been impressive if Mara cared about that kind of thing.

But she didn't. She couldn't.

She cared about winning her own gold medals. That was it.

"After I won that race, it opened doors for me, man. Doors that had money and opportunity and excitement behind them. My phone was suddenly ringing," Kirby continued. "'Do you want to be on this dating show? How about a social strategy show? A celebrity cook-off? The grandmaster of the Pride parade?' I couldn't believe it. It changed my life."

"And to the different networks and streaming services and events contacting you, you say?" Janette asked.

"Hell yes. Put me in everything. I'll do it all."

"Have you watched any of Kirby's shows, Mara?" Janette asked.

"No."

Yes.

"Why not?"

"I avoid empty calories," Mara bit out. Her anger was starting to wear thin, but she didn't want to come back to the real world. She didn't want to face it. She wanted to live in this moment that was hot and sharp and biting.

Kirby laughed at that, which shouldn't have made Mara feel like she'd won something, but it did.

"Reality TV is entertaining," Kirby said. "It's fun. And I love it. I love watching it. I love being on it. You'll never hear me call it empty calories or a guilty pleasure. Because I don't feel guilty about pleasure."

Janette whipped out a sheet of paper. "This is the list of shows you've appeared on: *Celebrity Dance Crew*, *Genius Academy*, *Celebrity BBQ Grill-Off*, *The Love Algorithm*, and *The Love Algorithm All-Stars*. There is no line on what you'll agree to do?"

"I mean, I'm not going to go to space for a bit of clout, but otherwise, gates are pretty wide open."

"Even if it disrupts your training?"

"I'm here, aren't I? I qualified. I made the team. I'm feeling good and gaining momentum this season at exactly the right time."

What had Kirby said earlier?

That was true but wasn't the truth.

The interview carried on without Mara for a few minutes. She had screwed up.

She'd been trying so hard not to make the same mistakes as last time in Beijing. She'd wanted to put her best foot forward. Maybe be a team player for once. Set the record straight by winning this time. And set herself up for after the Olympics.

Instead, she had let her own control slip through her fingers. And *that* would be the headline. A snippy cat fight with Kirby Bonham would be the headline. Again! It would be nothing but a distraction.

She couldn't imagine what Coach Karlsson would say. Or her sponsors. Or Chandler Wendleton.

Or her father.

Her brain couldn't fathom what all the strangers on the Internet might think. What they might say in disgusting, sexist comments. When would the interview be released? During the Olympics?

During primetime right before the fifty kilometer?

Right before she choked again?

Janette asked her a question, but Mara didn't quite catch it. "I apologize. Can you repeat the question, please?"

"Oh, there she is," Kirby whispered. "So polite. Back in control."

But Mara wasn't in control at all. She ignored Kirby and shaped her face into the mask she had perfected as a preteen when it had become clear she was special and gifted and going places.

Janette tried to get them back on course. Or maybe she tried to get them back *off* course. Mara wasn't sure. She treated the rest of the interview like the suffer fest it was. She put her head down and double-poled through to the end. She refused to say anything interesting, giving the rote, preplanned answers she should have from the beginning. Kirby's heart didn't seem in it once Mara stopped playing her game.

And that was exactly what had happened. Mara had tried to play Kirby's game and had come out the loser.

Again.

CHAPTER
SIX

THE INTERVIEW ENDED and the lights came on in the rest of the room, revealing all the camera people and staff. One of the reps from US Ski and Snowboarding was standing in the corner looking shellshocked.

Good.

Kirby wanted them to be. The longer the interview had gone on, the more heated it had become, the angrier at everyone she'd gotten. How dare they ask her to be nice and biddable. They might as well have told her to smile more. How insulting.

Chandler Wendleton caught her eye before storming out. He was great at the dramatic exit. It made Kirby laugh.

Janette smiled at them like she'd won the lottery. "That was certainly an interesting interview. Thank you both for being so vulnerable."

Vulnerable was a nice way to look at it. Kirby hadn't felt vulnerable, though. She'd felt powerful.

"Making headlines, making money," she said lightly,

shaking Janette's hand. And it was true. Brand deals, followers, TV shows. Good press or bad press. It all helped Kirby in the long run.

Kirby reluctantly glanced at Mara. Mara looked queasy, which almost made Kirby feel bad. But ultimately, Mara had snapped back in that interview just as harshly. She'd played her own role, and it had been incredible.

Mara's best self was not the uptight little ice princess. It was the badass who could take Kirby down a million pegs with sharp words. But no one seemed to see that but Kirby.

Kirby couldn't stick around watching Mara gape like a fish, so she bailed. Her body was buzzing. She had to get her pent-up energy out, and she knew the best way to do it.

She'd made it down one hallway, then another, before she realized she was being followed.

"Bonham!"

Mara's shout was an arrow to Kirby's chest. Kirby wanted to fight more, to push more, but she knew the fighting was already getting dangerously close to something else. Something tempting and complicated.

So she kept moving. Another hallway. Another turn, until she was fully lost.

"Hey!" Mara yelled again. "What are you doing? Where are you going?"

"To play Bunco. Where do you think I'm going?" Kirby said, not slowing down.

"Honestly, KB, I couldn't begin to imagine."

Kirby reeled back to Mara and trapped her against a white wall, backing her up with nothing but closeness. She didn't touch her, but she wanted to.

Kirby had two inches on her, and it was way too satisfying to see how Mara had to tip her chin up to glare at her.

They were alone again. It had happened more often in the past few days than the four years before. They were usually surrounded by coaches, trainers, nutritionists, and people whose sole purpose was to optimize their intervals, bodies, and mental states.

"You called me KB." Kirby lifted her hand, and Mara flinched. Kirby pressed her palm directly above Mara's shoulder, boxing her in. "Calm down. I'm not going to Nancy Kerrigan you."

"Everyone calls you KB. Even Janette Collins called you that." There was steel in Mara's voice and a stubborn set to her jaw.

"You don't." Kirby smiled and ever-so-gently tapped her fingertip against the curve of Mara's shoulder, trailing along the seam on her lime-green quarter zip. It was a ridiculous color, but it looked incredible on her. "You've always called me—"

"Bonham, stop it," Mara hissed and knocked Kirby's hand away.

"Bonham. Yep. There it is. So sporty."

"Stop."

"Last names. Handshakes and fake smiles when I beat you. No smiles when you beat me because you're too humble to be happy for yourself. But something got into you during that interview. It was hot, Mara May."

"Stop."

"Nah." Kirby was getting into dangerous territory, but there was such an appealing frigidness to Mara's glare, and

Kirby wanted to feel the burn of frostbite for a bit longer. "What do you need?"

"I don't—I don't know. It feels like you stabbed me in the back in there. Why would you do that?"

"I don't owe you anything. I control my own narrative, and I refuse to be a pitstop on the Mara May redemption tour. I won four years ago. *I did that.* But somehow your failures have fallen at my feet."

"It wasn't my idea. I didn't ask to do this interview."

"No. You just follow instructions."

Mara glanced away from her, and a bloom of red rushed over her cheeks. Kirby didn't want that. She wanted Mara's focus on her.

Kirby stepped closer, and Mara's gaze flew to her in surprise. Kirby could smell Mara's fancy fucking perfume again. She smelled rich. And good.

Mara could have ducked under Kirby's arm, could have stepped away at any point. She could have pushed past, and it would have been understandable. But she hadn't. She'd stayed right there.

"I liked it," Kirby said. "When you said KB. It sounds different when you say it. *Meaner.*" Fuck, she loved the way Mara's lips pursed in anger, the way she was breathing hard. All pissed off and hot as hell. "I'm going to go find someone to fuck."

"Excuse me?" Mara snapped, so polite even though politeness had flown out the window long ago.

"*That's* where I'm going. You asked. I'm going to find a hot, willing athlete in peak physical condition who also needs to burn off nerves and excitement and stress."

"But—" Mara seemed to glitch. She was frozen and looked so confused.

"But what?"

"We're not done."

"Mara May, unless you're finally gonna finger fuck me in this hallway, we are definitely done."

Mara's eyes went wide, and her gaze strayed to Kirby's mouth for a beat. Then a longer one. Then it was like her brain came back online and she snarled, "Why do you have to be so crass? I meant we aren't done competing. We still have a week until the Olympics and over three weeks until our events end."

"So?"

"You're going to start some type of relationship right now?" Mara said, her words tumbling over each other. "It will interfere with—"

"I find it very adorable you think I'm about to go have a grand romance. Trust me. It's just going to be hot and meaningless."

"We have training in three hours."

Kirby stepped back and shrugged. She couldn't believe Mara was even still there, engaging. "Again, I say, so?"

"You'll ruin your—"

"Appetite? I doubt that. It's pretty healthy."

"I was going to say *focus*."

"Ah. Worrying about your competition? How sweet," Kirby said.

"I'm not sweet, and—"

"Oh, I know."

"—you're not my competition."

Kirby had been feeling so smug. She hadn't expected something quite that cutting.

Mara continued, "When was the last time you raced a personal best? Hit a personal goal? When was the last time you cared more about winning than your follower count and TV appearance fees? Do you really think you can touch me? Or the podium?"

Kirby felt like she'd been punched. It wasn't any worse than the things she'd goaded Mara into saying in the past, but it did get to a particularly hidden piece of her heart. The fear that she *had* peaked in Beijing. That it was all a fluke. That she didn't actually belong and never would

"*Touch you*, huh?" Kirby said, her voice low. She was more pissed than she had any right to be. "What an interesting turn of phrase you chose there, Mara May."

Mara shook her head in exasperation. Or maybe denial.

"It feels good, doesn't it?" Kirby whispered when Mara didn't respond.

"What does?"

"Being nasty."

"I'm not—"

Kirby laughed, and Mara's mouth snapped shut.

"Maybe I won't medal. Or beat you. But at least I'm in charge of my own life. And I'll have fun. Fun skiing. Fun getting famous. Fun fucking. Fun fucking with you. When was the last time you felt true, unbridled joy, Mara? Do you ever let yourself be happy?"

"Toddlers feel joy when they see bubbles. What a ridiculous thing to ask."

"Winning a gold won't make you whole," Kirby whispered like she was telling Mara a really important secret.

If Mara had been a cartoon, smoke would have been billowing out her ears. She looked like she was about to rip the walls down around them, too worked up to even speak.

"Why are you playing by their rules? Following their scripts?" Kirby asked. She was going to control her own story this time. "You've already proven yourself, princess. Maybe you can let yourself have a little bit of fun. Maybe we both can."

Kirby couldn't help it. She touched a lock of Mara's dark hair that had fallen over her shoulder. Mara sucked in a sharp breath, turned on her heels, and walked away.

CHAPTER
SEVEN

KIRBY SET her phone up to record her, Apollo, and Lindsey to see who could do the most pullups. She and Lindsey were doing theirs with a fifty-pound weight tied to their waists, and she would post the video later that day.

Kirby knew where her bread was buttered. It wasn't in gold medals. It wasn't with US Ski and Snowboard or whatever narrative they had wanted to drum up about her and Mara May.

To them, Kirby was the villain. The class clown who had unexpectedly squeaked out a gold four years ago in the biggest upset in years.

She didn't train as hard as Mara. She didn't take herself, or skiing, as seriously. She lived a very fulfilling life outside of skiing. She didn't keep her mouth—*or legs*—shut. Or her queerness quiet. Or her opinions to herself.

And worst of all, she kept baiting Mara into lowering herself to Kirby's level.

But it felt pretty nice down at Kirby's level.

"Jesus, Kirby, why did you insist on filming this?" Apollo gritted out as they all pulled themselves up in unison, and Kirby snapped back into the moment. She had to stop thinking about Mara freaking May.

Apollo was going to drop first, which made every competitive bone in Kirby's body sing.

He let go of the bar and landed on his feet. Lindsey laughed and did one more rep before dropping as well. Kirby could practically see the comment section in her head as she did another rep for good measure before lowering herself carefully to the ground. Apollo helped her down and disconnected the weight from around her waist.

She leaned toward the camera, grinned, and made a funny face with her tongue sticking out. She would cut the video there.

She tried to make a video or a post every day to stay in the headlines and to keep the algorithms working for her. She didn't enjoy the social media aspect as much as being on television shows, but she did it for the money.

"I actually need to work out now," Lindsey said. It had been nice of her to do a video for Kirby. Lindsey was notoriously private. Her socials weren't even public.

"Sure, sure." Kirby gave her a hug. "Thanks for humoring me."

Lindsey smiled at Apollo, and he watched her walk away.

They were the only three in the weight room, which was odd. It was rare to get alone time. Kirby had been to the training center in Oberhof a million times since it was one of the US team's main European training hubs. It was just as much her home as anywhere else, which was to say, it meant nothing to her.

Apollo threw his arm over her shoulder. His tatted arm was heavy, and his skin stuck to hers. She was in shorts and a sports bra. They were both glistening from their warm-up run.

Tattoos. Bare skin. Sweat. Thirst for attention.

Hello to her bread and butter.

"All right, what's wrong with you?" Apollo asked.

"What? Nothing."

"Seriously, KB? You've been weird since you got back from LA. You don't usually ghost me."

She gritted her teeth. She hadn't told him about the interview.

Or about all the weirdness with Mara. That felt like a special little secret.

"I'm fine."

"Bullshit, baby. I saw you doing that breathing thing at breakfast, so I know you—"

"Don't call me that." She shoved him away playfully, even though she wasn't feeling playful at all. They fucked occasionally, but she was no one's baby. And she definitely didn't want to talk about "that breathing thing."

"I heard a rumor," Apollo said. He glanced over at Lindsey, who had her back to them.

"About what?" Rumors, gossip, drama. Typical for cross-country skiing.

"That you fucked up an interview, and everyone's pissed at you."

She scrubbed a hand over her face. "No one should be pissed at me but Mara."

Kirby and her agent had debriefed yesterday, and her agency was smoothing things over with everyone who needed to be smoothed.

"What did you do?" Apollo whispered. He didn't sound judgy, bless him. Just concerned for her.

"The usual. Opened my mouth and said the wrong things. But Mara followed suit, which was"—*amazing, wonderful, fun*—"maybe less than ideal. Chandler Wendleton could make my life harder if he wanted."

She squirted water into her mouth before jumping up to do another round of pull-ups. Apollo leaned against a pole and watched. There was no one more allergic to conditioning than Apollo.

Once she dropped, he said, "Who cares what Chandler Wendleton has to say? I don't even think US Ski and Snowboard cares. And they're not who matters anyway. Your teammates matter. Your coaches."

"Yeah, well, let's hope I haven't fucked up my place with my teammates and coaches then."

"You prove you deserve your spot every time you ski, KB. The other stuff is just noise."

That was true but didn't *feel* like it was. Some people didn't love that she made headlines and money for things other than skiing.

"You're my family," Apollo continued. "Nothing will ever change that. Even if you stopped skiing tomorrow. And Lindsey loves you. She let you win the pullup competition."

"Hey!"

"Brandilyn and Jordan would walk across hot coals for you. Coach Wu would burn the world down to help you."

Kirby shook her head. She hoped that was true. The fear it wasn't true, or wouldn't be one day—one day in the future when she said the wrong thing or lost the wrong race or let her fame-chasing go too far—was overwhelming.

Apollo grabbed her hand and squeezed. He *was* her family. It wasn't conditional. She had learned to trust that after years and years. He'd taken her home at Thanksgiving once when they were nineteen and she'd had literally nowhere else to go, and the rest was history. Found family had supported her much more than biological ever had, but it was hard to believe they would always be there for her. Even if she wasn't on TV. Even if she wasn't one of the best skiers in the world.

Tears bubbled up in her throat. She pushed them down and breathed through it.

She wasn't usually such an easy mark, but her emotions were all right at the surface. It felt like at any moment her brain might deceive her again, push her into another anxiety attack, and she wouldn't be prepared.

"Okay, okay, that's enough," Kirby said. She gave Apollo a side hug, and he kissed the top of her head, holding her close for an extra minute.

The door to the gym opened, and a physio came in. "KB? Coach Wu wants a quick chat."

"Uh-oh," Apollo sang under his breath. "Remember what I said. You belong. Even if you piss people off."

"If you say so." Kirby followed the physio to a hallway

of office suites. She was sure she was about to get a talking to. She'd been waiting for it all morning, but she'd hoped it would be from Chandler Wendleton, or the head coach, Coach Redman. Not Coach Wu.

She *cared* what Coach Wu thought of her. It mattered.

As she reached the door, Mara came out. They both pulled up before running into each other.

Mara was wearing pink, and her ponytail fell in a perfect waterfall of curls. Her Disney looks tricked people. They tricked the media and coaches and fans into thinking she was sweet. That she was the heroine of cross-country skiing.

It was all an illusion. A lie.

"So nice to see you, Mara," Kirby said.

Mara's eyes flashed, and a riptide of adrenaline hit Kirby full force. She braced for Mara's words. She couldn't wait to see what Mara did. What Mara said. How she reacted to something as simple as a greeting.

"Enough," Coach Wu said from the doorway, her voice wry. Coach Wu enjoyed Kirby more than most people, but there were limits. "Come in here, KB."

Kirby slipped by Mara and into the makeshift office. Coach Karlsson was also there, but he didn't glance up from his laptop as Kirby sat down. He had headphones on.

"You need to focus the fuck up, Kirby," Coach Wu said. No lead up or pleasantries.

Heat rushed over Kirby's face. "I will."

"Look, I get it." Kirby must have made a face at that because Coach Wu said, "No, really. I do. You have every right to push against anyone's effort to make you palatable.

I like that you do. I want you to have that chip on your shoulder. I want you to race angry. But no one should matter to you but you. Focus on your own training." Coach Wu tapped her own temple. "Get yourself together in here."

"I am."

Coach Wu shook her head like she knew that was a big fat lie.

"Stop letting her distract you," Coach Wu said, dropping her voice low.

Kirby sighed. "She's not."

"We both know that's not true. You don't have anything to prove to anyone but yourself."

"We both know that's not true," Kirby said, mimicking in the most respectful tone she could. "Did Mara get this same speech?" She looked at Coach Karlsson, but he either couldn't hear her with his headphones on or was pretending not to.

"Mara doesn't need anyone to tell her when she's fucking up. She does that just fine on her own."

"Okay."

"You'll be separated for the pre-Olympics press conference. They don't want to risk a repeat."

Kirby shouldn't have felt disappointed about that, but she did. She loved sparring with Mara. And the press conference before the Beijing Olympics had changed her life.

"That means we'll do press day individually?" Kirby asked.

"Mara will do hers individually. You'll do yours with the rest of the team."

So Mara was getting pulled out for special treatment. Classic.

Coach Wu leaned back in her desk chair and flipped a page in her notebook. "Now, let's talk about the team sprint. You'll be racing with Brandilyn and—"

"Wait, that's it?"

Coach Wu studied Kirby, and Kirby felt so *seen*. She wasn't sure she liked it.

"You and Mara are big girls. You both have agents who can help you determine media strategies. I don't give a shit about that as long as your head and body are where they need to be when you put your skis on. Understand?"

"Yeah. Hey, Coach?"

"Yes?"

"Thank you."

"Don't thank me. *Win*."

MARA WAS *PARTICULAR.*

After making her first podium in the World Championships, she wore the exact same necklace she had worn that day anytime she put her skis on. She fixed her hair the same for competitions—a tight French braid with a purple hair tie. She always wore her lucky lip balm, and she had different lucky lip balm for every event.

She had two pairs of sunglasses—a pair for training and a pair for competitions—plus one single pair with clear lenses for evening or cloudy-weather skiing.

Her dad called her irrational. But she liked to think she was intense. A control freak. She could control her jewelry. Her hair tie. Her socks. Her skis.

There was so much she had so little control over. Other people. The weather. The media.

Interviews with Janette Collins.

Her heart rate when Kirby touched her shoulder that one time.

Jordan and her puppy dog eyes when she asked Mara to borrow a pair of sunglasses before a warm-up ski with the whole team.

They were doing a nice, easy fifteen kilometers for conditioning. *Together*. To foster a team atmosphere. But everyone had been giving her a wide berth, just like she liked it.

After that hellscape of an interview, Mara wasn't in the mood to foster shit.

"I lost my sunglasses," Jordan said. Mara glanced between Brandilyn and Jordan. They were young. Nineteen and twenty-one. Younger than she'd been at her first Olympics even. "Do you have an extra pair with you? I'll give them back later, I swear."

Mara was shocked to be asked. Skiers were picky about their gear. There wasn't a lot of sharing. Hoarding was much more common, especially as the Olympics got closer.

"It's okay if you don't have any. Or if you don't want to lend them to me," Jordan said, her voice small. "I get it. I'm sorry for asking."

Oh, God.

"Here. Hold on."

Mara grabbed her competition pair out of her bag. They had a sunshine yellow rim. She put them on and handed her practice pair to Jordan. They were silver.

"Wow. Really?" Jordan said, staring down at the silver sunglasses like Mara had given her a diamond.

"Sure."

And it was fine. They finished their warm-up. It was

sunny, so it was fortunate Jordan had been able to use Mara's sunglasses.

But then Jordan took off with Brandilyn without giving them back. Mara didn't want to be petty and chase her down, so she took a deep breath and let it go. She would get them back that afternoon.

But when the afternoon came, and Mara showed up for her private training session with Coach Karlsson, Jordan, who was supposed to be there before her, wasn't there.

It was okay. It would be okay. Mara trained. She was smooth as butter.

Five days to the Opening Ceremony.

Six to her first event.

Everything might have been spiraling out of control off the course, but she'd never felt better in her skis.

She hit the intervals she was supposed to. Her legs felt good. Her breath was on point. She visualized every push, every curve and hill. She was laser focused, and it was a great practice. The best she'd had since arriving in Oberhof.

It was the type of training session that helped her put the interview behind her. To put Kirby and Kirby's games behind her.

But on the last turn, her sunglasses fell off. They dropped right off her face, one earpiece disconnecting from the frame. The sun glared off the snow, and she had to blink to adjust to the cold air and brightness hurting her eyes. She kept going because she was a professional. Shit happened all the time. She finished her session, recovered for a few minutes, debriefed with Coach Karlsson, and went back for the pieces of her glasses spread across the trail.

Jordan was stretching at the start of the course, chatting with Coach Wu, when Mara returned. She wasn't wearing Mara's sunglasses.

Mara marched up to them, the broken glasses in her fist. "Where are my sunglasses?"

Jordan jumped and everyone looked at Mara.

"Sorry for interrupting," Mara said, politeness springing forward like a defense mechanism. "Mine broke. I need my other pair."

Mara felt out of sorts and kind of pissed. It was probably a blessing in disguise that hers had broken during training rather than a race, but she couldn't help but feel like they had broken *because* she was wearing them for training.

"They're in my room. I forgot them on my bedside table. I'm so sorry."

"Okay." Mara's mind raced. She needed to get another pair regardless. She was sponsored by the brand but didn't have any of the extras they had sent her over the years. They were all at her condo in Anchorage. So she would need to buy a pair or find the team's cache of swag. But then which pair would be her competition ones? She wouldn't get a chance to make one of them lucky.

"I can go get them for you," Jordan said.

"No, you cannot. You have training right now. You can get them for Mara later. *Right*, Mara?" Coach Wu said, and Mara suddenly felt very silly.

"Of course."

"Here's my room key. It's room 2B. They're on my bedside table. Just go grab them, and I'll find you to get my key back later." Jordan practically tripped over herself to give Mara the key.

"Are you sharing with someone? Or are you staying with family?"

"Kirby. But she's filming something." *Of course she was.* "She won't be back until this evening, so you won't be disturbing her."

"Thank you. I'll get this back to you. I won't forget." Mara held up the key, and Jordan nodded with a bit of chagrin.

Mara showered quickly, threw on sweats and a tank top, and walked through an internal hallway in the apartment complex to Jordan's unit.

Her brain couldn't stop replaying her sunglasses flying off. Bad luck. Weird luck. Was it an omen?

She knew she wouldn't settle down until she was holding the other pair of sunglasses.

She keyed into Jordan and Kirby's suite. The team had booked all the skiers in a complex that was within walking distance of the training facilities and trails. Their apartments were nice, but Mara hated sharing. She could have insisted on renting her own apartment, *had* insisted on that in the past, in fact, but it was working out okay this year. She'd specifically asked to share with Lindsey, who she got along with better than most anyone in the world. And Mara felt more integrated with the team than in the past. She'd even walked to breakfast with Lindsey a time or two. And she'd shared her sunglasses. She was being a team player for once in her life.

Jordan's apartment looked identical to hers, so it was easy to spot the bedrooms off the kitchen and dining area.

Jordan had said the sunglasses were in her room, so Mara headed through the living room to the hallway, only to hear a gasp. She froze.

It was a sex noise. Her body knew it before her brain had caught up. But no one was supposed to be there. Jordan was training. Kirby was filming.

Supposed to be filming, at least, because as Mara flattened herself to the nearest wall, it became quite evident that Kirby was not filming but was in fact in her bedroom having sex.

Mara didn't know what to do. Her mind immediately reeled with images of Kirby twisting naked in the sheets with Apollo. There were rumors about them, of course. In fact, Mara knew of no fewer than five skiers Kirby had been rumored to screw around with. Mara pretended she was above that type of gossip, but obviously she wasn't.

Once, she'd seen paparazzi photos of Kirby kissing one of the women from that dating show she'd done years ago. Not the most recent dating show. The first one Kirby had filmed just months after the Beijing Olympics. Mara had kept that picture open in a tab on her phone for years. It unstuck something in her chest to look at it sometimes. To examine it. The way Kirby's hand gripped the back of the woman's head. The way she had seemed so carefree. It gave Mara something to direct her anger at. This picture of Kirby living her life while Mara's felt like it had fallen apart.

But now Mara let her brain go *there* instead. To Kirby taking apart that woman in the picture who had looked too perfect to be real. But Kirby was real. She was hot, and chaotic, and imperfect, and Mara had spent way, way too long trying to ignore that and failing miserably.

A moan filtered into the living room, and Mara's knees about hit the floor. She needed to leave. To put one foot in front of the other and get out of there. But she was rooted to the spot, her brain screaming at her to leave but her legs incapable.

A muffled "Oh, God" echoed through the thin walls, followed by a sharp, short cry.

Jesus, Mara had fucked up. She could not believe she had listened to Kirby have… She couldn't even allow herself to think the word.

What had she come here to get?

It didn't matter. She had to leave.

As soon as she could draw a breath. As soon as she could move without passing out.

Fight or flight or freeze.

Her body chose for her, and it was *freeze* all day long.

The bedroom door slammed open, and Mara thought for one, blissful moment that Kirby wouldn't see her as she waltzed out in plaid pajama shorts and a bra holding a sex toy in one hand, clearly heading to the bathroom.

A sex toy.

As if from a distance, it clicked that Mara had not heard anyone else. Just Kirby. Maybe Kirby was alone.

Was that better? Or worse?

Kirby jumped when she saw Mara standing there, but she recovered as quick as a cat.

"What are you—"

"I came to get—"

They spoke at the same time. Then stopped at the same time.

Something like anger burned in Kirby's gaze.

"I'm sorry," Mara said. The apology felt sticky in her mouth.

"For what?" Kirby prowled toward her, and the room started spinning again.

Kirby had thigh tattoos—a coiled snake on one leg and swirling florals on the other. Mara had seen them in TikTok videos and in the locker room. But she had never looked closely. She wanted to look closely.

"For listening." Her words shocked her, probably shocked them both.

Kirby didn't stop until their bodies were almost touching. Mara closed her eyes.

She'd fucked up. She'd fucked up. She had no idea what was about to happen, but she had never been so embarrassed.

"Did you like listening, Mara May?" Kirby whispered, danger soaking her voice. Mara could feel the heat from Kirby's skin.

She was about to cry, and she couldn't remember the last time she'd cried.

No, wait. That wasn't true. She'd cried after losing the gold to Kirby by the thinnest margin. A photo finish. Mara had cried right there at the finish line, barely able to breathe, collapsed on the ground from exertion, her whole body in pain. She'd seen her teary face as a gif once. Crying publicly had made the humiliation so much worse. She had nightmares about it. She was known as an emotionless skier. She rarely fell to the ground after races. She didn't show what she was thinking or feeling—the good or the bad.

She never allowed herself to cry. She'd locked that part of her heart off. She'd put it on ice.

But tears pricked at her right then, threatening to make another appearance.

Kirby dropped the sex toy. It was bright orange. It thunked to the floor. Mara flinched and looked up.

Their eyes locked, and for one brief second, neither of them moved or breathed. They just gazed at each other.

And then Kirby was on her. Against her. Kissing her with a desperation that sunk every shred of resistance Mara would have normally mustered.

Instead, she melted under Kirby's touch, her searing kiss. The sweep of her tongue. It was rough and a revelation.

"Tell me," Kirby snapped, ripping her mouth away from Mara's before kissing her neck. Mara gasped, and her spine seemed to go liquid. "Admit it."

"What?" Mara managed.

"You liked it. Liked hearing me fuck myself. You're not as innocent as everyone thinks."

"I don't—I'm not..."

Kirby grabbed Mara's hair, wrapping the long fall of her ponytail around a fist. "Do you want to kiss me back, Mara May?"

Mara tried to lean forward, to show her answer rather than saying it out loud. Kissing Kirby Bonham was a terrible idea. It was ruinous, if Mara were being perfectly honest with herself, but she would do anything to get back to Kirby's magic mouth.

Kirby's tight fist in Mara's hair held her head against the wall, making it impossible for her to move. It should have been embarrassing, trying to get her mouth back to Kirby at Kirby's demand. Not being able to move because of Kirby's grip in her hair. But it wasn't embarrassing. Not at all.

Not yet, at least.

"God, look at you." Kirby pressed her thigh between Mara's legs, right against her center, and Mara couldn't help it—she thrust, grinding against it one time. "That's it. Feels good, huh?"

Mara should have felt shame, but she didn't feel anything but a wild, spiraling need. She nodded.

Kirby pressed harder, leaned in and bit her earlobe. "I'm gonna wreck you, princess," she whispered. "Lick." She lifted her thumb to Mara's lips, and Mara obeyed.

Obedience and submission weren't her usual MO during—Jesus, she couldn't even call this sex. It was more of a hormonal car crash.

But the whirlwind of it all, the shock, the longing that she'd pushed down for so long was breaking like a dam. She was breaking.

"You want this?" Kirby asked against her mouth. She slipped her hand under the band of Mara's sweatpants but didn't go farther.

Mara nodded again.

"Use your big girl words," Kirby demanded, her voice

still mean and so hot Mara gasped. "Mmm, I like your dirty sounds, but I want words."

"Yes."

"Yes, what?"

"I want you to—"

Kirby kissed her harshly for half a second. "Stop there. Stop at 'I want you.'"

"Okay." Mara was wet. Her clit was throbbing. She needed so little to come and wanted so much. "I want you."

"Good."

Kirby shoved Mara's pants and underwear down to her thighs. She dragged her thumb over Mara's clit and through the center of her pussy, gathering up all that wetness in one sweep.

Mara threw her head back. It banged against the living room wall. She hadn't moved her feet once. She was still planted in the same place she'd been since she'd heard Kirby masturbating in her bedroom.

Kirby grabbed one of Mara's boobs over her shirt and squeezed it, making a feral noise in the back of her throat that sent another throb through Mara's whole body.

"Love your tits, Mara May," Kirby said, voice gravelly. "You're coming apart, and I'm barely doing anything."

Shame mingled with Mara's horniness in a way that just made her feel hotter and more out of control. Kirby circled Mara's clit a few times with her thumb before twisting her hand and plunging fingers inside her. Mara clenched, wanting more. It was so good, and she moved her hips, trying to impale herself deeper on Kirby's fingers.

"I want..."

"*You,*" Kirby snapped. She tugged on Mara's shirt, trying to lift it up, but with only one hand, it didn't work.

Mara whipped it off. "I want you."

If she was going to crash the car anyway, she might as well unbuckle and go all in.

"Fuck yes." Kirby nipped Mara's shoulder and slid the front zipper of Mara's sports bra down until her breasts were free and the bra was hanging open.

Kirby spread all the arousal from between Mara's legs to her clit before pressing her fingers inside again, her thumb strumming a quick, slick rhythm.

"I want you," Mara said. Then Kirby licked Mara's nipple into her mouth.

Mara was a breath away from coming, her body tight and shaking. Kirby sucked on one nipple before switching to the other and biting down.

And Mara finally allowed herself to touch. She delved her hands into Kirby's short wavy hair, held her to her breast, and arched toward her mouth. "Oh, no. I want you. *I want you.*"

That pinch of pain, the fast and furious thrust of fingers, the flick of a thumb on her clit—it shattered her. And she came harder than she ever had in her entire life.

THAT HAD CERTAINLY BEEN... something.

Kirby had screwed up. It wasn't an unusual feeling for her after sex. She was kind of known for bungling things in that arena. Notorious for it even. As multiple TV shows had exhibited. But there was something extra messed up about it happening with Mara fucking May.

Mara hadn't opened her eyes since she'd come. Kirby hadn't even been completely sure that Mara was into women. Kirby had suspected—their weird, angry sexual tension wasn't just in her head, obviously—but Mara's sexuality wasn't a topic she had spoken about in interviews. There were no rumors about her dating women.

Or anyone.

"Here, sit down."

Mara jumped at Kirby's voice, and her eyes flew open. They were so green up close. Unfairly green. Her face was blank.

"It's okay," Kirby said. She pulled Mara's sweatpants

back up for her. Mara swallowed hard and sank to the ground, and Kirby followed her down.

"Jordan borrowed my extra sunglasses. Then mine broke during training. I think that might be a bad omen." Mara sounded dazed.

"All right." Kirby nodded like that was relevant in any way.

"I was coming to get my extras. Jordan gave me her key card. I need them to ski. Superstition."

"Sure."

"Umm. Should I, *you know*?"

Leave? Kirby certainly hoped she didn't. This was a disaster, but Kirby wasn't ready for it to end.

"Should you what?"

"Reciprocate?" Mara's lips twisted like she was uncomfortable, and Kirby nearly laughed. She stopped herself, but it was close.

"No. It's fine."

"Oh. If you don't want me to, okay." Mara's chest rose with a quick breath. And another. God, she was so fucking pretty. "But I can. I don't want to leave you…"

"Hanging?"

"Yes."

Kirby should not touch her again. She absolutely should not. But she was going to.

She lightly touched Mara's chin. Forced Mara to look at her. Mara let herself be led, and Kirby's lizard brain lit up.

It had been so good. The fast, furious clash of their bodies had been *so good*.

"I already got mine," Kirby whispered. Mara's breath sped up even more. "You listened, remember?"

"I'm sorry about that." An apology. How novel. Neither of them had ever uttered those words to each other about anything.

And Mara's voice was so, so soft it was almost impossible to hear. But Kirby could feel it, feel the words against her lips as she closed the distance completely.

Their lips barely brushed. A sweet, real kiss. Different than the aggression of the sex they'd just had. Mara trembled, and Kirby pulled back to watch.

"That was probably a bad idea," Kirby said.

Mara's expression went through about three emotions, all too fast for Kirby to get an accurate read. "The kiss or the…?"

Kirby was surprised Mara wasn't running away as fast as possible. One of them needed to pump the brakes. Mara was the responsible one, no doubt, but Kirby wasn't delusional. This was not a good idea, and at any second, Mara was going to turn back into a block of ice.

"I think both."

"Yeah." Mara stared over Kirby's shoulder. "I would have liked to have, you know."

"No. What would you have liked to do, Mara?"

Mara sighed and zipped up her bra. "Reciprocate."

Kirby almost reached over to drag that zipper right back down. She had been trying to be respectful and not a complete horndog as Mara came down from the personality transplant that had allowed her to let loose a little bit. But now that those beautiful breasts were hidden again, Kirby was ready to throw a fit.

And that one word—*reciprocate*—was so brave. Kirby had danced, strategized, cooked, and dated on TV for money. She had raced and taken tactical risks while skiing.

But she was never brave when it mattered. Mara's courage touched Kirby, made everything realign in her mind about what had just gone down.

"Next time?" Kirby said. Throwing out a line, seeing if Mara would bite.

It was a terrible, terrible, brilliantly terrible idea. And Kirby would do it every fucking day if it meant she got to see a daring Mara again. They simply had to keep their emotions out of it.

Easy for Mara the ice princess. Maybe not so easy for Kirby, who ran hot and fast and reckless.

Mara rolled her head loosely against the wall, which might have been a *no* or a *what the fuck have I done?*

But she didn't respond. That was common, Kirby realized. For Mara to not answer questions when the questions were hard.

Mara closed her eyes and took a shaky breath. "When was the last time *you* felt joyful?"

Kirby blinked, her mind spinning, and let herself look her fill at Mara while her eyes were shut. She'd asked Mara that days ago. Mara had seemed so stunned by the question. Like it had hurt her.

Kirby almost said *when you let me kiss you.* But that was much, much too vulnerable. And today, Mara was the brave one. Not Kirby.

"I don't know. Last time I went dancing maybe." She had line-danced at a queer cowboy club in LA a few months ago. It had been a blast. So uncomplicated and jubilant.

Mara wrinkled her nose and opened her eyes.

"You don't dance?" Kirby asked.

"Of course not," she said like that was the most obvious thing in the world. "I think winning is the closest I get to joy."

That was a very Mara response, but it was also sad.

"What about when I made you come on my fingers?" Kirby asked, trying so hard to be brave, but mixing it all up in dirty talk. "Did that spark some joy, Mara May?"

Red exploded over Mara's cheeks, and she put a hand to her forehead. After several long seconds, she said, "I don't feel like myself right now."

"Gotcha." *Ouch.*

"I shouldn't have liked that."

"Hey, there's no *shouldn't have* here. We're adults. We're both single." Kirby's stomach dropped. God, she hoped Mara was single. "Right?"

"Sure." Mara moved her hand away from her face and looked at Kirby with a resolve that reminded Kirby of Mara's game face before a race. "I can't do that again."

Fair. That was fair. Just because Kirby's brain was reeling with possibilities and reciprocity and regrets and excitement and plans didn't mean Mara's was. Kirby felt all the things, but it wasn't fair to expect Mara to feel anything at all.

Kirby cupped Mara's cheek. Another risk. Mara didn't

lean into her palm, but she didn't pull away either. "It's okay. You can't be anyone but yourself."

That was the big question mark, though, wasn't it? Kirby didn't know Mara. She suspected no one did.

Mara's eyebrows dipped at that, and her eyes moved like she was reading Kirby's words from a book in front of her and didn't like the sentence structure.

Kirby needed a minute to breathe. She stood up and left to grab Mara's sunglasses from Jordan's room. Jordan and Brandilyn had acted like they were holding a Fabergé egg when they had shown Kirby Mara's glasses earlier. Kirby had told them that Mara would need those back ASAP. Mara always wore the silver ones for training, and Kirby had no idea how or why she knew that, but she did.

Kirby found the glasses in Jordan's room, snatched them off the bedside table, took a deep breath, and marched back into the living room. Mara had put her shirt back on and was about to bolt.

"For you." Kirby handed the sunglasses over. Mara grabbed for them like she was trying not to touch Kirby's fingers.

The glasses tumbled to the ground, and Mara looked stricken.

Kirby quickly bent to pick them back up. "They're fine. Here." She stepped forward, and Mara tensed, which made defensiveness rise in Kirby's throat like acid. She hadn't done anything wrong here. Neither of them had. But it hurt that Mara was acting so jumpy about it.

Kirby placed them on top of Mara's head like a headband. Their eyes met as Kirby stepped back.

"I won't tell anyone," Kirby said. Kirby didn't usually hide her hookups, but she assumed that Mara wasn't thrilled by the optics of having sex with Kirby.

They were rivals. Kirby had beaten Mara in her best event the one time it mattered most. They had just had a contentious interview that would air during the Olympics.

And that wasn't even touching the personality issues. Kirby was rough around the edges. Loud. Messy. Vulgar.

Probably the last person Mara would have chosen to spend time with outside of skiing. Or inside of it.

But it had been incredible.

Mara kind of shrugged, all awkward and clipped. "Thanks for…"

Kirby set her jaw and nodded her head toward Mara's hair. "The sunglasses."

Mara stared at her hard, taking in every bit of Kirby's face for one, then two uncomfortably long seconds. Then Mara turned on her heel and left.

MARA HAD BEEN to Val di Fiemme and the ski center in Tesero a million times, but it felt different with the Olympic glitz and glam all over everything. She wanted to enjoy the Olympics this time around. To really take it in, to live in every moment, but that wasn't how her brain worked.

Her mind had been running timelines for weeks, and the end dates were fast approaching.

Only two days to train unhindered by competition.

Only three days until the Opening Ceremony.

Only four days to practice perfecting her transition from classic to freestyle for the skiathlon.

Only nine days to the ten-kilometer freestyle race. After that, there were ten days before the fifty-k to rest up, replenish, and get her head on straight.

The schedule had become a mantra she repeated to calm down.

Two days. Three days. Four days…

But new timelines were vying for attention.

Forty-two hours since walking into Kirby's apartment.

Forty-one since Kirby had said, *You can't be anyone but yourself,* in a way that made Mara feel like *herself* didn't measure up. They hadn't spoken since.

Twenty-four hours since Mara watched Kirby's pre-Olympics press conference. Kirby hadn't mentioned her once, which bothered Mara even more than when Kirby insulted her.

Two hours since they'd been in the same room during breakfast in the smaller Predazzo Olympic Village, but they might as well have been on different continents.

Their hookup had been nothing but a minor hiccup in the grand scheme of their lives.

It was par for the course for Mara not to talk to Kirby. For them to orbit each other without a word exchanged. They had spent most of their careers in that mode, with small detours when they crashed together in the press.

But that secret hour two days ago had consumed every corner of Mara's brain that wasn't already consumed with skiing. And quite a few that should have been consumed with skiing as well.

It wasn't like her. When she allowed herself to have romantic or sexual exchanges, the mental toll was minimal. Matters of the heart came in around twentieth on her list of things to worry about. Below important stuff like nutrition optimization, summer roller skiing, and the HOA bylaws at the Anchorage condo she rarely spent time at.

She'd never let a random hookup affect her skiing.

Mara had caught glimpses of Kirby at training, and of course, she looked better than she had in ages. Precise but loose too. Smooth. Like she'd hit a stride. A sweet spot.

Mara didn't feel like she was in the sweet spot at all. She felt restless, tight, and out of sorts. She should have been meditating. That was what was on her schedule for that morning. But instead, she was staring up at the ceiling of her double room as her phone buzzed again and again.

Lindsey, her roommate, was watching a show with Apollo on her phone. They were sharing corded earphones, which seemed more intimate than just about anything Mara could imagine. They hadn't made a peep, but Mara couldn't quite ignore that they were there.

She glanced at her phone. It was her dad.

Still.

It had been fifteen days since she'd talked to him.

It had been one hour since she'd ignored his first call. Half an hour since she'd ignored his third.

It rang again, so she picked it up. It was better to deal with her father than to turn the experience with Kirby over in her brain for the thousandth time.

"Hi, Dad," she said after picking up. "What's up?"

"Oh, she lives," he said, all sulky and put upon. Raymond May had perfected that tone long ago and used it to great effect.

"Yes."

"I'm available for the next two hours, so we should get coffee."

Mara closed her eyes. "You're already in Italy?"

It wasn't surprising. Her father had figured out ways to

exist in cross-country skiing circles for her whole life, but he was one of those people who didn't keep a job for very long. It was never his fault of course. When she'd last seen him, he'd been in the vendor village, consulting for a popular wax brand who had sent him to Goms, Switzerland, for the World Cup events there. So maybe he'd been hanging out in Europe since, waiting for the Games to start.

But she'd thought both her parents planned to arrive, separately, the day before the Opening Ceremony.

"Yes, I've got a new opportunity in the hopper with a junior Nordic team who need—"

"And you want to get coffee?" Mara said, interrupting the long spiel that was coming.

"I only have two hours, so you'd have to cancel whatever Ulf Karlsson has you wasting time on today," he said. Because of course her Olympic training wasn't as important as his "new opportunity in the hopper."

"I'm free until this afternoon anyway, but I'll have to factor in time to get back through security at the Olympic Village."

"Why are you staying in the Olympic Village? You could have acquired nicer accommodation without the—"

"I'll send you an address to a nearby café and see you soon," she said and hung up.

Mara sent him the address for a café some of the athletes had walked to yesterday, and whizzed by Lindsey and Apollo, who didn't even acknowledge her presence.

Her dad was waiting for her at a table right by the front window. Raymond May was tall, fit, and intense. He had a way of staring right through a person. For most of Mara's life, his voice had been the main one in her head, telling her what to do, how to train, what was important, what wasn't.

It was a hard thing to change, but after the Olympics four years ago, with the help of therapy, she'd started retraining herself. She'd had to pick herself up and put herself back together after the embarrassing defeat in the thirty kilometer and poor showings in the other Olympic events. What she'd needed from her dad was for him to be a dad, not a coach or consultant or ski support. She'd brought Coach Karlsson on board as her main coach, working with him through phone calls and texts when they weren't in the same place. His voice was the one she wanted to hear when it came to skiing. Coach Karlsson's voice and her own.

Her dad hadn't forgiven her for it. He didn't seem to know how to be a dad without also having a say in her skiing.

"Have you spoken to your agent this week?" he said before he'd tasted his coffee. He was wearing a Team USA–branded beanie. "Now that you insist on paying that fancy agency, they should have you booked and busy. I heard Kirby Bonham filmed two commercials last week."

Mara forced floaty blankness to take over her brain. It was the only way she managed speak to her father these days.

He was a bulldozer. He had always been her biggest supporter and her most aggressive critic.

She loved him. It was complicated.

She passed him a packet of sugar to pour into his coffee. She took a sip of her smoothie. The coffee shop they'd met at was busy. She'd already had to sign several autographs, which only happened to her in big European cross-country skiing hubs or at the Olympics. She occasionally got recognized in Anchorage, but Alaskans typically gave her space. Liking their space was baked into most Alaskans' DNA.

"We filmed all my sponsorship stuff weeks ago. I wanted to take these past few weeks to focus on training, not commercials."

How he knew about Kirby's filming schedule was anyone's guess. He probably followed her Instagram account. Hell, he probably had Google alerts set up for Kirby's name.

Mara had deleted social media apps off her phone after the first impulse to look at Kirby's TikTok after their hookup.

Kirby posted every day. Sometimes multiple times a day. Mara had wanted to see if Kirby had seemed happy in the posts following the sunglasses incident. Had she seemed as dazed and anxious as Mara felt?

But she didn't have the time or the mental energy to obsess over it. So she'd removed any and all online temptation.

Instead, she just looked and looked and looked at Kirby every time they were in the same space. For two days. No words exchanged. No recognition.

Which was good. That was for the best.

"What interviews did KB get booked for?" her dad asked, snapping her out of a spiral.

"How would I know that?"

"Well, don't you talk?"

Mara tried to keep her face from changing but failed.

"What, Mara?" her dad asked loudly. "Have something to say?"

"*Dad.*"

"Yes?"

"Of course I don't know Kirby Bonham's interview schedule. I'm assuming she got a lot of the same calls I did. The pre-Olympics press day was yesterday. I took questions on my own." She was sure it had been the most boring press conference ever, and she'd actually missed being there with the full team. "We filmed an interview with Janette Collins together."

It was better to give him a heads-up to hopefully decrease the eventual reaction. Because that interview had not been boring.

"Why would you do that?" he asked, his voice incredulous. Honestly, that was a fair question.

"I wanted to."

It was more complicated than that. She'd been asked to, and it had felt wrong to say no. It was hard to turn down a primetime interview with a premiere Olympics correspondent.

But also, she'd wanted to take advantage of the legacy-building opportunity, the chance to *be* the princess of cross-country skiing. It had been a tactical error.

"How was the interview?"

"Interesting."

"Hmm. Okay." He gave her that judgmental once-over she was so used to. "Have you seen this?" He held up his phone. A Facebook reel started playing with no sound.

It appeared to be a podcast interview between a man and Kirby, their screens split. Kirby was in her room in Oberhof. They were both smiling and laughing a lot.

"It's muted," she said as mildly as she could, even as dread trembled through her.

Seeing Kirby smiling, laughing, and looking gorgeous made Mara's heart thump in her throat. She had felt different since their *incident*. Like what they had done was permanently marked on her skin. She couldn't believe every person she'd interacted with hadn't been able to look at her and know.

"There are subtitles."

Mara took a deep breath and pictured a pond of calm water. It was all she could do to keep from seeing red.

"I didn't read them." The video had cycled to a new clip of cats playing with a cardboard box. Her dad's Facebook algorithm was truly a mystery.

He sighed in exasperation and fiddled with his phone to get back to the video. "Listen to it."

"I'm not going to listen to a video in the middle of a coffee shop without headphones."

"Jesus, Mara. Why are you being so contrary? She bashes you."

"Let me see." She snatched the phone from her dad and held it up to her ear.

The man's voice filtered through. "And what about Mara May? What is your strategy in a race with her?"

Kirby says, "Ah man. Don't ask me that. You'll get me in trouble."

Mara frowned. She wasn't sure what she'd expected.

She glanced at the screen and could see it was from a podcast called *Arctic Out and About.* There was an Alaska state flag and a progress Pride flag in the background. Kirby chatting with a queer podcast from Mara's home turf rubbed her all kinds of wrong. Not that they would have ever thought to invite her to their podcast. Being unapproachable and private had that effect.

"You like trouble, though," the man said. "That's what you're known for!"

Kirby laughed, which made Mara's breath catch.

"You caught me. Fuck, okay. Keep her within your sights. Then she gets too confident or too gassed and bang, champagne toasts and gold." There was a weird blip like words had been cut. Maybe the host's next question. "She's perfectly fine. But unless it's about ski gear or trail conditions, we don't have anything in common. Mara is… *hmm,* how do I say this nicely? She's a very self-contained and unflappable human being."

"Are you saying she's boring?" the host asked. "I feel the need to defend my fellow Alaskan."

"Have you ever met her?" Kirby asked. "I've heard Anchorage described as the biggest small town."

"I saw her on the trails once. I waved."

"Did she wave back?" Kirby asked, delight evident in her voice.

"No."

They both cracked up at that.

"Well, *boring* is your interpretation, not mine." Kirby's tone was the equivalent of a shrug.

Mara handed the phone back. It was impressive how

Kirby had managed to make something so bland sound so mean.

"That wasn't too bad."

"You don't care at all that she's talking about you?"

"It's a pointless video."

"Has"—her dad turned the phone around to look at the screen—"*Arctic Out and About* asked to interview you?"

Mara pinched the bridge of her nose. She almost felt like laughing. "No."

"You're a better skier. You should be getting these interviews. Plus, you're, *you know.*"

"Gay?"

"Well, yeah."

"She is the defending gold medalist in the thirty-k. She's the only American cross-country skier to get a gold in Beijing. Kirby is flashy." Heat rose up her neck.

Mara had learned Kirby was lots and lots of things. Flashy was just one of them.

"You're flashy. You dress like… that." Her dad gestured at her pale-yellow sweatshirt and matching sweatpants. His opinion of it was quite clear in his tone.

"Yes. I have a sponsorship deal with this brand. Because I like wearing these colors."

Compartmentalize. Deep breath.

"You should be getting more interviews, Mara Louise. More than her."

It hadn't taken long to be first and middle named. As much as her dad tried to be a coach, he always reverted to dad voice eventually.

"I am."

"With who?"

"The usuals, Dad. It's fine. I don't like being interviewed. I'm happy with what has been arranged."

Well, she wasn't happy with the way the interview with Janette Collins had gone.

Except she kind of was happy with it.

It was complicated.

Kirby had been right that it had felt good to let loose. To stop hiding her true thoughts and feelings. And Kirby wasn't holding back when it came to talking about Mara.

"The narrative should be that you're—"

"Stop it." She shook her head, one quick jerk, and her dad's mouth snapped shut. He seemed shocked, and Mara felt a short, sharp pulse of happiness at that.

A mom and her preteen daughter walked up right at that moment with an athletic bag for Mara to sign. They were American. The girl, Avery, had a pair of sunglasses pushed up on her head that looked like the ones Mara had broken during training.

"Did you get your sunglasses here in Predazzo?" Mara asked as she signed the bag. "I broke a pair this week and need another."

"You can have these," Avery said, much too eagerly, and practically threw the glasses at Mara.

"Oh, no. That's not what I meant." She had honestly just been trying to make small talk. "Here." Mara took the permanent marker and drew a tiny heart on the inside of the earpiece of the sunglasses. "Think of me when you wear these and are going really fast."

They were a favorite brand of most cross-country skiers,

and Mara could have tossed a stick and hit a store with them in stock.

The girl stared at the heart and seemed to get emotional, which Mara was not equipped to handle at all.

"Who's your favorite skier?" Mara blurted out. It was a question her agent had taught her to ask when she had to chitchat with fans. People usually said *Mara May* because it would be rude not to say your favorite skier was the skiing superstar right in front of you. But preteens didn't always have their social etiquette dialed in because Avery didn't miss a beat. And she did not say Mara May.

"Kirby Bonham."

Mara blinked. Her dad's mouth dropped open. The girl's mom closed her eyes briefly.

"What?" Avery said. She peeked back at her mom, seemingly confused or maybe defensive about everyone's reaction. "Kirby has a gold medal. And she won *Genius Academy*."

A laugh bubbled its way out of Mara, and she couldn't swallow it. She would never escape Kirby. "Of course she did."

The young girl's mom also laughed, a bit nervously perhaps, but still a hearty chuckle.

Mara's dad did not.

"I like you too. Obviously," Avery said sullenly.

"Sure."

"And you'll probably win gold this time. And then you'll be, like, even."

"Okay, Avery. Let's go," her mom said.

"It was so nice to meet you, Avery," Mara said. She was having trouble keeping her laughter inside. Mara would never win *Genius Academy,* so she and Kirby would never be *even.*

And Kirby had won a gold first. She'd always have that over Mara.

Four years ago, the television networks, sports journalists, and the team's media department had decided she deserved to be coronated once she won the gold. They had built it up. She had let them.

Then she hadn't won the gold after all.

And *that* had been the story. A failed Olympics. A failed gold medal.

Hubris didn't make you a star, but it did occasionally get you roasted by a preteen in an Italian café. What was it that Kirby had said? Mara got too confident at the end. She hadn't felt confident since losing in Beijing. That loss was a constant stitch in her side, reminding her to be humble, to try hard, to push and fight and win.

Once they were alone, Mara's dad said, "See?" like that whole interaction with the young girl had proven some big point.

A point about her. A point about Kirby.

Mara stood up to order something, *anything,* else.

While in line, a protein bar in hand, something Kirby had said during their hookup snuck up on her.

Use your big girl words.

A blush so hot it felt like flames burst over her face, but she turned the sentence over in her head anyway.

There was no reason that phrase should have been as

sexy as it had been, but Mara had really, really liked the frank meanness. The bite in Kirby's tone.

Mara paid for her protein bar and another coffee for her dad. She returned to their table.

"Here's a coffee." She placed it in front of him. He didn't thank her or look up from his phone.

"So you're not racing in any of the sprint events?"

"No." She did fine in sprints and had won bronze in the sprint in Pyeongchang, but they were not her best events by any stretch.

He shook his head in disbelief. "And your training regimen involves an hour of yoga and meditation every day? That's what this article says. I'm not sure that's the best use of your time. I know Coach Karlsson thinks the optimal way to train is a mix of low-intensity—"

"My training is off-limits."

"Excuse me, Mara Louise?" Oh, there was the dad voice again.

Big girl words. Big girl words.

Mara wanted to be brave. To set the right boundaries, not the wrong ones. She was pretty sure she had set the wrong boundaries with Kirby.

But she was going to fall apart if all she heard every time she talked to one of the most important people in her life was that she was lacking and needed to be doing more. The voice in her head did that enough.

"Give me this time to focus without you in my ear second-guessing everything, and I'll see you once I'm done competing."

"In nineteen days? You're not going to see me for nineteen days?" he said, referencing how many days remained until the fifty-k.

"Correct."

He put on a hurt expression. "You used to value my opinion."

That wasn't untrue. Her dad had always been *around*, more than everyone else's support networks. He had helped her stay insulated, focused.

And she had needed that. Wanted that. Thrived that way.

But insulation and isolation were starting to feel pretty similar. And if this was her last experience, her last shot at Olympic gold, it was time to do things differently.

"I love you, Dad. But I'm not entertaining this type of, I don't know, debriefing with you right now."

Big girl words.

"I've never known you to be ungrateful," he said. She braced for a lecture about the insane amount of time spent, the money, the sacrifices. "But it's your choice. I don't need to stick around just to bear witness to your mistakes."

And that was the rub, wasn't it? She *was* racking up the mistakes, one after another. The interview, the sunglasses, the loss of focus, Kirby Bonham.

Doubt trickled through her brain. What if he was right? If everything fell apart, would she look back at this moment and wish she'd exhausted herself racing all six events? Would she wish she'd made more money with appearances and sponsorships prior to the Olympics? Would she wish she had molded the media story around her in a way that benefited her more?

Maybe it would have been better to do extra commercials and press. To hit the princess narrative harder.

Her dad stood up, and she jumped. She felt upset.

"Guess I'll give you that space," he said.

She nodded. "Don't forget your coffee."

He snatched it off the table and walked away.

CHAPTER
ELEVEN

THE LAST PERSON Kirby expected to knock on her door was Mara May.

"Can I help you?" Kirby asked, trying to infuse her voice with some teasing. It had been days since they'd spoken, and Kirby wasn't quite sure what attitude she should bring to this interaction.

Mara didn't bite at the joking tone. She said, "Is Jordan here?"

"No. She's over at the training center. Why?"

"I bought her glasses." Mara held up a shopping bag from a high-end Italian sporting goods store.

"Wow. That's nice of you, which is… odd. You know most of us have sponsorships with—"

Mara slipped by Kirby, entering the room completely uninvited, leaving Kirby standing in the doorway gaping at air.

"Okay." Kirby followed Mara. "What are you doing?"

Mara tossed the bag onto Jordan's bed, the sunglasses rattling.

"What's this?" Mara held up her phone. A video started to play, but it was muted. It was from a queer outdoor and winter sports podcast she had done a few days ago. It had been a casual chat. Kirby knew they were going to post clips soon, but she hadn't seen any yet. The host had asked her a million questions, from how she felt about the new equal racing distances for men and women ("big fan of equality"), to her opinions on the current political climate in the US ("fuck those hateful fuckers"), to her thoughts about her main opponents.

Uh-oh.

"It's muted," Kirby said.

Mara made a very unladylike noise and tossed her phone onto Kirby's bed. "You know what you said."

"Yeah." Kirby didn't exactly regret it. The podcast had been the morning after their hookup, and she'd chosen to talk about Mara as if she hadn't just secretly had sex with her. It would have made zero sense if she'd acted all polite. And she hadn't said anything too terrible.

"Is this what we're doing now? Slamming each other any chance we get?" Mara snarled.

"Feel free to slam me back. You're capable of backing it up. And you secretly like being vicious, so let it out, princess."

Mara had avoided Kirby for days. No eye contact. No smiles. Zero acknowledgment. The usual treatment from her, honestly.

Except they'd fucked.

So this whole interaction was like bizarro world. None of it made sense. Not Mara showing up at her door. Or going straight to Kirby's bed brandishing her phone like a weapon. Not Mara bearing gifts.

And definitely not Mara stripping her shirt off in one fluid move.

"I want to do things differently this time around. The Olympics, I mean," Mara said. "I want to enjoy myself. Make friends. Be a good teammate."

What the actual fuck was happening? If this was Mara being a good teammate, Kirby was a fan.

"Okay," Kirby said slowly, but Mara wasn't listening. She was ripping off her socks.

"So I bought Jordan sunglasses. Even though she probably already has some. It's silly."

"No, it's not."

"I'm tired of being so… angry and alone."

"Right."

"But I *like* being angry with you."

"That's a bit dysfunctional, Mara May… which is my jam."

Mara was in nothing but pants and a sports bra. She started to take the pants off, and Kirby finally got herself into gear. Mara had made this decision. To come to Kirby. To take her clothes off for Kirby. An offering. A question.

Kirby stalked around the bed and finished the job for Mara, yanking the pants down. Mara stepped out of them, and stood there, all defiance and discomfort in a bra and panties.

Kirby shoved her back onto the bed. "This what you need, Mara May? A distraction?"

Mara nodded. Her eyes were wide like maybe her actions were catching up with her.

Kirby grabbed her ankle. "A distraction from the very true things I said about you on some podcast with limited reach."

"It's going viral."

Kirby doubted that. Mara just had no idea what viral actually meant.

"Anything else?" Kirby asked. She pressed her lips to Mara's calf. "Anything else you want a distraction from."

"My father."

"Ah, daddy issues. Hot."

Mara almost—*almost*—laughed and Kirby almost—*almost*—felt like she'd won a gold medal all over again.

"What do you want?" Kirby asked.

"I don't know."

"What do you like?"

Mara huffed and closed her eyes. Kirby was losing her. Giving Mara too much time to second-guess and freak out. But sometimes you had to wade through the logistics to get to the good part.

"I have a great bill of health and get tested often. Just a little FYI," Kirby said. She kissed the inside of Mara's knee.

"Okay."

"Sexual health."

"Yeah. I got that."

Kirby smiled. "This is the part where you could also tell me about your sexual health status if you wanted."

"Oh. Right. It's fine. I'm… Everything was fine on my last physical. And they did… all that."

"Good." Kirby laughed. Mara was one of the most frustrating people on the planet, but Kirby found her incredibly endearing right then.

Mara sat up and looked at the door. "Umm. So."

Yep, Kirby was definitely losing her.

Kirby grabbed Mara's ankles and yanked, which toppled Mara onto her back.

"How about this?" Kirby tugged a special bag out from under her bed. It was a bag she always traveled with. She pulled out the first sex toy she touched. "It's my turn. Make me come and maybe I'll return the favor."

Mara was a go-getter. She needed a task.

Kirby handed over a toy called the Clitapult, a name she assumed was related to its resemblance to the throwing arm of a catapult. But it was quite simply a clit-sucker toy. A very effective one.

"I don't even know what to do with this." Mara held it up, aggravation eating up her words, but Kirby knew—and she didn't know how she knew, but she did—that it was a front. A façade. A part of this game.

And that was absolutely what this was. A game. Kirby saying something mean on a podcast had been foreplay. This was the main event.

Kirby slid her track pants down and off. "Well, time's ticking. I'm seeing the, uh, the physio in an hour." That was a fib, but it wasn't Mara's business that Kirby was meeting with a sports psych. That was personal. More personal than getting naked together. "You better figure it out."

To help Mara along, Kirby took off her briefs too, so she was in nothing but a tank top. She lay back on the bed, folded her hands behind her head, and bit her lip on a smile.

Mara rolled her eyes, tossed the toy beside Kirby, and knee walked until she was between Kirby's legs.

Then she shocked the hell out of Kirby by pressing those insanely hot lips to Kirby's clit.

A jolt rocked through Kirby. She was sensitive, and honestly kind of easy. Sometimes too easy.

"You ever do this before, Mara?" Kirby said from between gritted teeth. She didn't know why she asked that except she wanted to hear Mara talk about her experience. Because stuff like that turned Kirby on. Making Mara talk to her turned her on.

Mara gave Kirby a slow, hard suck before lifting her face away. "No. I'm just an innocent little princess, remember?" Disdain dripped from her voice.

Kirby grinned and reached down to fist Mara's long hair. "Don't get snotty with me."

"Or what?" Mara rolled her eyes again.

She was really leaning into the bratty thing. Or was she actually bratty?

Kirby had no idea.

And it didn't matter. Kirby's reaction was the same either way.

It was *hot* either way.

She yanked on Mara's hair, forcing her back a few inches.

"Fuck me with your fingers."

Mara followed her orders, but she still had that stubborn set to her jaw. Kirby loved it.

She loved the tentative touch, the way Mara quickly got more assertive as she realized how much Kirby liked it. Mara tried to lean back toward Kirby's cunt, but Kirby wouldn't let her, holding her by her hair.

"Fine," Mara grumbled as she sat up. Kirby let her, not willing to keep Mara in place if she truly wanted to get away. But Kirby quickly realized Mara's intention as she picked up the Clitapult.

Mara looked at it like it was a ridiculous waste of time but also kept up a steady finger fuck with her other hand. She touched some of the buttons on the toy. It buzzed to life, softly at first, then louder as she upped the intensity.

Honestly, Kirby could have come just from Mara's fingers in her pussy. It was almost inconvenient how close she was. She wanted to draw it out. Make Mara keep working for it. But if she used that toy on Kirby on *that* setting, it would be over.

"Start low," Kirby managed to gasp out, but the words were clipped and didn't really make sense. Or at least Mara pretended they didn't make sense.

"What?" Mara pressed the head of the Clitapult, set on a higher setting, over Kirby's clit in the most nonchalant way.

Kirby had managed to stay relatively in control to that point.

But she lost all semblance of control in three seconds flat. She moaned and jerked, her body inadvertently shying away from the intensity of the toy.

"Oh," Mara said like she'd discovered something surprising.

And that was the last thing Kirby heard besides her own babbling. "I'm gonna—turn it—oh God, Mara."

Mara fucked her harder with two or maybe three fingers and kept the toy pressed firmly against Kirby's clit, and Kirby tried to hold in her scream as a sharp, hard orgasm ripped through her.

The light in the room sparkled in her vision, and she couldn't stop rolling her head back and forth against the bed. She was being loud. Too loud. Not smothering her sounds at all anymore.

"Too much," Kirby panted and pushed the clit sucker away, but Mara didn't let up with her fingers, and more pulses, softer ones, throbbed through Kirby, her body squeezing Mara's fingers again and again.

Kirby felt uncomfortably thrown.

She sat up and glared at Mara. Mara glared back before a smile started to slip over her sinful lips.

Kirby grabbed Mara's wrist and licked her taste off Mara's fingertips. Then she manhandled Mara onto her back and bit the inside of her thigh.

"Oh, so you *are* going to return the favor after all?" Mara said, and she had every right to sound smug, but it still pissed Kirby off.

She wrapped her arm over Mara's hip and pinned her down with a hand on her stomach. And then she tasted her. For the first time.

Kirby had fooled around with her fair share of people. She knew that sometimes bodies just spoke to each other. A magnetic thing. Maybe a pheromone thing.

But no one had ever tasted as amazing as Mara. No one had ever smelled so good. Or felt as incredible.

Every once in a while Kirby pulled out the bells and whistles. The handcuffs. The vibrators. The strap-ons. She liked that shit. She liked bells and whistles.

But sometimes, nothing was better than good, old-fashioned head.

Mara moved against her mouth, her body chasing and pushing for everything all at once. Kirby lightly pinched her hip and lifted her mouth away.

"Calm down."

Mara had an arm thrown over her eyes. "How the heck am I supposed to calm down when you're going down on me? Jesus, don't be ridiculous."

"Stop pushing. Relax."

Mara pulled her arm off her face and sat up on her elbows, her abs rippling in a way that made Kirby want to lick her everywhere.

Mara clearly had something to say about those instructions, but Kirby didn't let her. She sucked on Mara's clit again and watched as Mara's head slammed back like she'd been punched.

"My bed is going to smell like you. Like whatever expensive perfume you wear all the time. Do you know how unfair that is?" Kirby said quietly.

Mara's mouth opened, but she didn't make a sound.

"Let me take care of you."

Mara shook her head, her eyes squeezed shut.

"I'll get you there."

"I know."

"Then what's the problem, princess?"

"Don't call me th—" Mara jerked as Kirby ran fingers through the wetness between Mara's legs. "Ah… please."

"Please, what?" Kirby swirled her tongue over Mara's clit and pressed her fingers inside. Mara's body quietly went wild. It was an intense thing. She didn't cry out. She barely moved. But the tension in her body ratcheted up like a bow that had been strung way too tight. "What, Mara?"

"It's been a long time. So hurry up."

A thrill raced down Kirby's spine, and she pressed her hips to the bed. She could go again. She could do this all fucking day. They were endurance athletes after all. The trouble they could get up to in this bed.

"It's only been two days," Kirby said.

"That doesn't count."

"Like hell it doesn't."

Mara made a growly, exasperated noise and tried to grab Kirby's head, but Kirby laughed and dodged her.

Still, it was time to put Mara out of her misery. Kirby dipped her mouth back to Mara's cunt and flicked her tongue over Mara's clit for several long minutes.

"You taste good."

"Ugh, shut up."

"No." Kirby licked right through the center of Mara's pussy. Mara had finally stopped chasing her orgasm. She was letting Kirby's machinations sweep over her. Giving Kirby the reins. "When was the last time someone did this for you? Took care of you like this?"

Mara rocked with the thrust of Kirby's fingers. "Harder. Please, harder."

It wasn't an answer to her question but did tell Kirby so much she wanted to know. She fucked Mara harder, sucked her clit harder for ten, twenty, thirty seconds, before pulling off.

Mara thumped her fist against the bed.

"When, princess? Tell me."

"God, I don't know. A week ago. They were better than you. Made me come so fast. Felt better than what you're… *Oh, fuck.*"

Kirby laughed at the way Mara was trying to bait her. It was a lie. Mara had just said so. But Kirby liked games.

She curled her fingers inside Mara's cunt, and it was like she'd found a ripcord and pulled it. Mara's body pulsed hard once, twice.

On the third pulse, Kirby licked Mara's clit again, and Mara detonated against her mouth, in her hands. Waves of pleasure rolled through her. She was silent through it all, but her body did the speaking. And Kirby loved what it had to say.

"SO ARE we going to do this whole"—Kirby flicked her hand around to indicate the bedroom after about five minutes of silence—"bullshit dance again?"

Mara didn't know what Kirby thought was bullshit. Their hookup? The possibility of a future one? Or the debrief afterward?

Mara stared at the ceiling and tried not to panic. It looked like the ceiling in her room. The room she'd escaped that morning, but this one smelled like sex. Jordan could return at any time. They hadn't kissed. On the lips, at least.

"Why did you say that about me?" Mara said instead of asking Kirby to define *bullshit* like it was a word in a spelling bee.

Can you give me the definition? Language of origin? How about using bullshit *in a sentence?*

"What do you mean?"

"On that podcast," Mara said. "Why did you say that?"

Kirby scrubbed a hand through her messy hair. "I can't remember exactly what I said. Was it bitchy?"

"It felt pointed."

"Let me see."

Mara picked up her phone, and Kirby scooted closer. She wrapped her legs in Mara's like it was the most natural thing in the world. Their naked skin pressed and slipped together. It was the closest to cuddling Mara had allowed herself in quite a long time.

They watched the video together. It was annoying how gorgeous Kirby looked. The camera loved her.

"That was the answer to two different questions," Kirby said mildly. "And the first answer was basically a compliment. I said the best strategy against you is to wait for you to get tired at the end. Which is true. And usually you don't get tired, so who cares that I said it."

"That is not a compliment, Bonham."

"And the rest is true. We don't have much in common, and you are unflappable. I didn't figure you wanted me to go on a podcast and say I had recently gotten to know your clit quite well."

"Can't you just stop talking about me altogether?"

"Don't you get asked about me constantly?" Kirby said. "I can't make it down the street without your name being shoved in my face and asked for my opinion."

"I don't do as much press as you," Mara said. She almost managed to keep her hatred of "doing press" out of her voice.

Kirby laughed. "I like that part of it. The interviews and shows and attention."

"Yeah, no kidding."

"That doesn't make me less than you. It doesn't make you better that all you care about is the love of the sport and blah, blah, blah." Kirby blunted her words by running her fingers through Mara's hair, starting at the temple and brushing a long line all the way to the tip of Mara's ponytail.

"I don't think it does." Except Mara maybe kind of did?

"More bullshit. It's really piling up."

Mara sighed and sat up. She didn't know why she had come there.

Well, that wasn't strictly true. She had been upset and antsy and mad. And she'd wanted to feel good again.

She hated to admit it, but Kirby made her feel good. At least when they were fooling around. The aftermath left a lot to be desired.

She'd told herself that she was there to confront Kirby about the podcast, to talk *again* about how to handle all the attention and media moving forward. To come up with a game plan like Kirby had originally asked for.

But instead, she had taken off her shirt.

"I know it's hard for you to understand," Kirby continued. "You've spent your whole life chasing golds and skiing greatness and all that shit. I've spent my whole life trying to scrape myself together. I can't squander this moment. I have to seize it because it might be the last one I ever get. I have to set myself up for whatever comes next."

"You don't think we're all doing that?" Mara said, suddenly madder than she had any right to be. "None of us can compete forever. We all have to plan for the *after*."

"Your after is going to look a lot different than mine."

"That was your choice. You chose to do the TV shows and the Instagram TikTok influencer stuff. You milked your gold for fame. You could have—"

"Melted into the background like a nice, compliant little woman?"

"Is that what you think of me?" Mara asked, breathless and hurt. "That I'm compliant?"

Kirby made an exasperated noise. "God, why can't we just have a normal conversation, Mara? What do you want me to do? Refuse to talk about my gold medal? Say something else nasty in the hopes it sends you right back into my bed? Because honestly, I'm quite enjoying that."

"That's not why—"

"You sure?" Kirby sat up too. She wrapped a tendril of Mara's hair round her index finger. "I don't mind. I don't mind if you show up every time your daddy makes you mad. Or I hurt your feelings by saying the most innocuous things ever in an interview. Or you have a bad practice. Or you break some sunglasses. I can be your anger management, baby. No biggie."

Mara moved away. The teasing in Kirby's voice pricked at her, made her stomach hurt. But also, that offer felt dangerous. It wasn't safe to want it so badly.

She needed to focus. To get her head on straight.

Kirby fell back on the bed and watched Mara as she got dressed. Kirby was still half-naked, and Mara forced herself not to look.

"That's it?" Kirby said as Mara put her shoes on.

"What do you mean?"

"You blow in here like Hurricane Mara, rip your clothes off, then act like I've done something wrong by making you come so hard you scream."

"I did not scream."

Kirby laughed. "Yeah, you mustn't let yourself vocalize what you like even for a second, huh?"

Jesus. Sometimes Mara really hated Kirby.

"We can't do this again," Mara said, loathing in her voice.

"No shit." Kirby laughed, but it sounded off. Forced.

"Racing is the most important thing. We both need to focus on that."

"I have been, princess. You're the one who keeps coming here."

Sick embarrassment dropped Mara's stomach because that was so, so true. She mustered up as much blankness as she could before responding. Compartmentalization. She was a pro at separating herself from her emotions.

It served her very, very well while skiing. Not so well while fighting with her biggest rival after an ill-advised hookup.

"It won't happen again," Mara said as coolly as possible. And then she left.

CHAPTER
THIRTEEN

KIRBY SKIPPED her session with the sports psychologist. She wouldn't be able to hide what had just happened. If she got there and started talking about the panic attacks and the anxiety and all the shit she had been hiding, the scarier secret—the Mara May secret—would come pouring out.

It would catch up with her. She assumed she couldn't say, "Hey, I need to talk about my mental health," then ghost said mental health professional without someone checking up on her. But that was a problem for later.

For the past few months—no, the past few years—Kirby had told herself that the most important thing was the other stuff. The TV appearances, the fame, the notoriety. Her bread and butter. It kept her bank account in the black. It gave her a nest egg. Skiing was what made her famous enough to find fame in other more lucrative ways.

She still raced at a high level. She won races. She won

money. She worked her ass off, worked harder than most people she knew because she managed it all while also doing reality TV like it was a full-time job.

She sat up straight in bed. Energy buzzed through her. She needed to do something. She spied the bag with the sunglasses on Jordan's bed.

Ridiculous.

Mara May was ridiculous.

Kirby looked into the bag and realized Mara had bought two pairs and labeled them. An all-black pair had Kirby's name on it.

Jordan's had baby pink rims.

Fuck.

Kirby called Apollo. Didn't even think about it. She felt ready to fly apart, and the only person she could imagine talking to was him.

"What's up?" He sounded half-asleep.

"What are you doing?" she asked.

"Uh… Hold on." There was whispering on the other end of the line. When he spoke again, he seemed more alert. "I'm just chilling."

"With who?"

"Lindsey," he said.

"Oh. Really?" That was new and fascinating information. "Were you guys taking a nice nap together, or…"

"Yeah, *or.*"

Kirby loved gossip. Loved knowing secrets and matchmaking. Apollo was her best friend, and she wanted the very best for him. Lindsey was one of the most solid and genuinely kind people she knew.

"How interesting."

"Look… Slow your roll there, KB."

"How long has that been going on?"

"Umm. Can we chat about this later?"

"Maybe while we ski? I need a break."

"Yep. Skate skis or classic?" he asked.

"Classic."

"Sweet. I'll be there in thirty. Are you okay?"

"Not really." It was the second time she'd admitted that out loud in just a handful of days. That should have felt like progress. Or like she was doing the right thing. But it felt like ripping her own skin from the muscle.

"I'll be there fast."

"See you soon."

An hour later, she and Apollo were on a trail. It was a local Predazzo flat loop trail that Coach Wu had suggested because they didn't have access to the Tesero Cross-Country Skiing Stadium except during specific time slots. They went at a leisurely pace, enjoying the wind on their faces and sun in their eyes. She didn't often get to ski for fun during competition season. She skied to train. She skied to practice, to optimize, to get better.

It had been a long time since she and Apollo had gone out together for no reason other than enjoying each other's company. They synced their earphones so they both could hear the same music. He let her choose, which meant they were listening to what Apollo called "wispy sapphic Americana." Not exactly pump-up music, but it made Kirby feel like she was in a movie with dramatic, beautiful needle drops.

After a few kilometers, Apollo paused the music and took out his earphones. Kirby did the same.

"Should we start with Lindsey?" Kirby asked.

"Sure."

"What's going on?"

He slowed to an easy glide. "I'm in love with her."

"What? You tried to get me to sleep with you like two days ago."

"It was longer than two days ago." He smiled. "I've been shooting my shot with Lindsey for five years. She rarely gives me the time of day. Except when she does."

"Wait, go back to the beginning."

"It's not all my story to tell."

"Apollo, stop being cagey. Just tell me what is yours to tell. And why is this the first I'm hearing about it? I tell you everything."

"You tell everyone everything, including TV viewers. That's your thing. I'm not special in that regard."

If she hadn't been worried about injuring him, she would have shoved him into the snow.

He smiled when he caught the dirty look she was giving him. "We went on a few dates five years ago. We hook up every couple months. Once a year maybe. But she lives in Park City and trains in Anchorage, and I split time between Vermont and Norway. She doesn't want to do long distance. I don't want to live in fucking Utah or Alaska. She gets boyfriends or starts dating other people, and I respect that and give her space. Then when they break up, we see each other, and fireworks, *bang*."

"You bang?"

He laughed, his beautiful, booming laugh. "No, I meant, like *bang*, we reconnect, and it's, I don't know, electric. Bang was for emphasis. Not an active verb."

"Okay, nerd. And you're in a bang cycle right now."

"Please don't ever say bang cycle."

"Lindsey seems so normal. I would not have expected her to be your type."

"What do you think my type is?"

"Well, *we* fool around occasionally, and I'm—"

"A drama queen."

Kirby ignored that. "And you slept with Tommi Korhonen, who is like a hot older ski daddy, last season."

Apollo picked up the pace. His cheeks were rosy, and Kirby didn't know if it was because he was wind chapped or embarrassed.

"Moral of the story, I don't have a type," he said. "Except Lindsey. *She's* my type."

Kirby was a little miffed that this was the first time Apollo had shared his feelings for Lindsey McGrath. But everyone had secrets.

"Your turn," Apollo said as they climbed a steady slope.

Kirby took a deep breath. "I decided I want to win."

"That's new?"

"Kind of. There's this narrative that I can never top Beijing. That it was a fluke."

"KB, you've won or hit the podium in the thirty kilometer multiple times since then."

"I've only beaten Mara three times. Plus, I'm not racing thirty kilometers this time. It's fifty."

"Okay, wait, wait. I'm not going to argue with you

about whether you, a gold fucking medalist, are a good skier. Why did you decide you 'want to win'? Which, I'm going to ignore how insane that sounds, but all right."

"Mara pissed me off."

Apollo slowed again. His variable speeds were starting to annoy her.

"And that's different *how*? She's been getting under your skin for four years."

"Not like this."

He glanced at her. "What did Mara do?"

Kirby shook her head. "It doesn't matter. I want to beat her."

"That's a relief to hear," he said very slowly. "I also want to beat the other skiers in my events. Glad to know you now realize how competition works."

Kirby came to a dead stop at the top of a hill, and Apollo zoomed past, tucking in as he descended. It took him several seconds to realize she was no longer beside him. He snowplowed to a stop, then duck-walked back up to her.

"Sorry," he said.

"For what?"

"Teasing you."

She looked up at the sky above them. It was robin's egg blue with cartoonishly fluffy clouds. She adjusted her new sunglasses.

"If I want it, it hurts more if I don't get it," Kirby said.

Apollo nodded, his eyebrows tipping down. It was such a basic statement. One that most people probably reconciled when it came to their dreams before they made it through puberty.

"That's the cost of hope, Kirb."

She smiled. He was the only one who called her that.

"So what should I do?" Kirby asked.

"Hope. Try your best. That's all you can do. All any of us can do. And stop running yourself ragged thinking about Mara May. She'll beat you or she won't. She'll win a gold or she won't. That's not your trauma. Worry about your own story."

"My story?"

"Yes." He nudged her with his elbow and started skiing again. She followed.

"I'm not sure I know what I want that to be anymore."

"Really? I thought the"—he waved a pole toward her—"you know, spectacle had a purpose. You told me you wanted to set yourself up for after the Olympics."

"Spectacle."

"The drama in the press with Mara. The TikToks. The everything. It's purposeful. It's a plan, right? You don't want to tell US Ski and Snowboard's story. You don't want to tell Mara's. Or the TV networks'."

"Yeah. I guess. *No*, you're right."

They skied through the trees until they hit a clearing with a large vista of the beautiful mountains. Apollo stopped again and leaned on his poles.

"What happened with Mara? What did she say? I didn't think she had given another interview."

"Nothing. She just…"

Apollo stared at her. She stared at the mountains, not willing to give him an inch because everything would come tumbling out. It would be worse than if she talked to the sports psych.

Kirby slipped a hand from her pole strap and took off her sunglasses to rub a smudge off them. Black rims. Black lenses. They were beautiful. They felt so right.

"She's nice, I think," Kirby said. "Nicer than she lets on. But she makes me so mad. Every time I'm around her, I feel like I'm coming out of my skin. Like I can't hold it together. And I'm already barely holding it together. It's an additional, I don't know, variable that I hadn't planned on."

"Well, you don't have to be around her. You're not friends. You rarely train together. She's spent her career hiding from her fellow skiers. It should be easy enough to avoid her."

"You're right. And I can win."

It felt like opening her chest to say that and mean it. To strip out the protective layers she'd shored up around herself that shielded her from the pressure and the exposure and the pain of competing in front of the world.

She needed to stop hiding behind her other self. The Kirby who did TV shows and went viral and made headlines. That person would still be there once this was over, regardless of the outcome.

"Anyone can win. That's the magic of the Olympics. But if you win another gold, it won't be a fluke, no matter what the ski snobs say. You have as much right to be here, to be *there*, in the very top echelon, as anyone else."

"Even if I'm just a queer redneck from Minnesota." She ground the tip of her pole into the snow. He had to know what buttons he was pressing. All the ones that kept her up at night and made her chase fame and security and attention.

"Especially as a queer redneck from Minnesota."

CHAPTER
FOURTEEN

MARA WOUND her way through several hallways to reach the suite of offices in the United States' block in the Predazzo Olympic Village. She needed to retrieve her Opening Ceremony uniform.

Because the Olympic venues were spread out throughout Italy, they were having smaller satellite Opening Ceremony events in every Olympic territory. She had to decide whether to attend in Predazzo or hire transportation to Milan and back.

One option was the responsible choice—staying in Predazzo—but, in her heart, she really wanted to go to Milan. She wanted to be where the biggest spectacle would be.

For some reason, spectacle was more appealing than ever before.

When she reached the right hallway, Kirby was sitting on the ground outside the office. She had earphones in and was studying something on her phone.

Mara's heartbeat took off like a shot. It happened every time she saw Kirby now, this unstoppable physical reaction. Her body just completely betrayed her, and she couldn't control it.

Kirby must not have heard or seen her approach because she didn't look up from her phone. As Mara got closer, she could see that Kirby was watching a race. It was the very first fifty-kilometer race in the World Cup after the distance changed from thirty kilometers to fifty.

Mara loved the change. She loved endurance. Loved pushing herself to the limit for kilometers upon kilometers. Cross-country skiing was a full-body sport. It was so physically demanding and *hard*. There was a reason skiers collapsed after crossing the finish line. It wasn't dramatics. It was exhaustion. And she was so good at overcoming the pain and fatigue, pushing through it to win.

She had come in second in that race, which had helped her clinch the World Cup Crystal Globe, but the race itself had been a battle of wills. The conditions had been terrible, the snow like mashed potatoes, and every skier out there had been suffering.

"You come in nineteenth," Mara said. Kirby startled and glanced up. She took an earphone out of one ear.

"What?"

"You come in nineteenth."

"I know where I placed, Mara May. I was there."

"Why are you watching that?"

Mara watched race film too but usually with her support team and Coach Karlsson to identify pain points or things to work on.

"Because I'm a masochist, obviously. Coach Wu told me to consider my strategy in deteriorating conditions. So I'm studying."

"Ah. Okay." It was hard being close to Kirby after everything. Mara wanted to be even closer and also as far away as possible. "What are you doing out here?"

"I'm here to pick up my outfit for the Opening Ceremony."

Mara sat down beside Kirby. "Me too."

"Lindsey's in there now."

On the screen of Kirby's phone, Kirby was passed by skier after skier before crossing the finish line and crumpling onto her back. She smacked the ground in frustration.

"That was a good result," Mara said.

"For you." Kirby was holding herself rigidly, which was strange. She was usually all loosey-goosey and relaxed.

"For you too. You're a sprinter. That was a great finish." And Kirby had placed higher in subsequent fifty-kilometer races. Truthfully, it was disingenuous to call Kirby a sprinter. She wasn't *just* a sprinter. She had worked hard to become well-rounded in the longer distances. But Mara knew it bothered Kirby to be labeled like that.

"I'm the Olympic gold medalist in that event, Mara," Kirby said flatly.

"That was thirty kilometers, though. Not fifty. It's different."

"No shit." Kirby flipped her phone between her fingers. Her hands were shaking.

"Are you okay?"

"Where's your favorite place to ski?" Kirby asked

abruptly, dropping her phone into her lap. She scrubbed her hands over her cheeks like she was trying to rub feeling back into them.

"My favorite place to compete?" Mara asked.

"Not compete. *Ski.*"

"I've never thought about it. Weather, elevation change, trail conditions, snow totals. They're simply variables to consider and plan for."

Kirby spun from her butt and sat up on her knees, facing Mara.

"No, not *compete,*" Kirby said again. "Where is your favorite place to just be you with the snow and trees and polar bears, or whatever it is you have up there in Alaska." A small tremor ran through Kirby's right hand, and she clenched it into a fist.

Mara frowned. "What's wrong with you?"

"Nothing. Answer me."

"God, I don't know, Bonham. Do you have a favorite place?"

Kirby shrugged and closed her eyes. She held her breath for several seconds before letting it out. Then she did it again.

Mara snapped her hand out and grabbed Kirby's wrist. Kirby gasped but didn't open her eyes.

Mara turned Kirby's wrist over, noticing that Kirby's hand was cramped into a claw.

"What's happening right now?" Mara whispered. She checked the hallway to make sure they were alone. "Are you sick?"

Kirby gave a sharp shake of her head and finally met Mara's eyes. "I'm fine. It doesn't matter."

That was so clearly not true. Mara felt almost scared by how untrue that was.

"Don't do that."

"Do what?"

"Lie."

"I don't know why…" Kirby took a harsh breath. "It's not like you care anyway."

"What do you mean by that?"

Kirby clenched her jaw, the muscle popping over and over. "Nothing. God, talking to you is worse than the breathing exercises."

"Hey," Mara said, voice frosty. Kirby flinched and looked up at her.

Kirby's eyes were blue, and her eyelashes were so long. And she had a scar under her eyebrow that Mara had never noticed, but now she wanted to run her thumb over it again and again.

With slow deliberation, Mara rubbed Kirby's wrist and palm in a great sweep. "There's this trail in Kincaid Park in Anchorage."

Kirby nodded and matched Mara's breathing. "I raced there for Junior Nationals once."

"Right. Well, this trail, Mize Loop, it's one of the first trails you learn to ski as a kid. It's easy. But it's my mom's favorite. She's not, uh, very comfortable on skis, but we ski it every Christmas morning. If we're together. I think it's the only time all winter she gets her skis out."

"That's nice. I haven't seen my parents in years."

"I know," Mara said gently. She rubbed Kirby's hands harder, pressing against Kirby's palms with her thumbs. "Do I need to get Coach? Or a doctor?"

Kirby grimaced and shook her head.

Mara stood up and helped Kirby up too. "Come with me."

Mara led Kirby through the facility, keeping her hands to herself but staying close to Kirby.

They found an empty hallway with an empty bathroom. Mara pushed Kirby through the door.

"There are no polar bears in Anchorage," Mara said. "Except at the zoo."

Kirby laughed, but it sounded loud and unnatural. "What?"

"There aren't polar bears where I grew up. They're farther north. Alaska is big."

"You're such a know-it-all."

"You need to slow down your breathing. You're hyperventilating."

"I know," Kirby said, her voice paper thin. Her breathing sped up. She was shivering.

"Tell me your favorite place to ski," Mara said. She slipped her hands up and down Kirby's arms.

"You've touched me more in the last five minutes than when we fucked."

"Hush. That's not true."

"Almost makes the panic attack worth it."

Mara ignored that. "Come on. Tell me your favorite place."

"Apollo and I skied out and camped in this primitive

yurt thing once in Vermont. I spent the weekend breaking trail in the wilderness and exploring. Then we skied into this little town with a dive bar, got drunk, and had a three-some with a hot bartender." All of Kirby's words rushed out in one big breath.

"That tracks."

"My lips are numb." Kirby squeezed her eyes shut. "They start to tingle and then my cheeks tingle. And then I get so sweaty. This is the worst. I'm sorry."

"You don't need to be sorry."

"It's embarrassing. We're competitors, and this feels like showing you every weakness I have. Oh, God," Kirby started to bend over like she was going to put her head between her legs.

Mara caught her and didn't let her. Then Mara's thumb was right there. Right on Kirby's bottom lip. Trying to rub the sensation back into it.

"I already know your weaknesses, Kirby."

A pained noise worked its way out of Kirby's throat. Mara would have done anything to take that pain away.

"Will you kiss me?" Kirby whispered. "Please. It was so good when you kissed me."

"Kissing isn't going to fix hyperventilation."

"It might. Nothing else has worked so far. Worth a shot."

"This happens to you often?"

Kirby nodded. Then shook her head. All contradictions. Her hands trembled as she reached for Mara's waist. They weren't cramped anymore. "More often recently."

"Match my breathing, Bonham."

"I liked it when you called me Kirby."

"Okay, Kirby."

Tears welled in Kirby's eyes, and Mara felt like she might come apart herself.

"I'm sorry," Kirby said again.

Mara pressed closer until Kirby would be able to feel the up and down of Mara's chest against her own body. Feel her breaths. The slow in and out.

"That's it." Another long slow sweep of her thumb over Kirby's lips. Then she raked her fingernails through Kirby's hair.

They breathed together for several minutes. Kirby relaxed in increments until she was a puddle against Mara.

Mara had never had a panic attack, but she knew they could wipe a person out, so she held Kirby up.

Kirby put forward such a vibrant, carefree image to the world, and she was tough. To come up in the ski world without familial support—monetary or otherwise. To compete at such a high level. To support herself through whatever means necessary and set herself up for the future. Mara might not have agreed with Kirby's career decisions, but there was no denying she was a hustler. Kirby possessed an incredible degree of mental and physical fortitude.

And if occasionally it all got to be too much for her, well that was understandable.

Kirby's arms snaked around Mara's waist, holding tighter than before when they had seemed rather limp.

"So the kissing is off the table, then?" Kirby asked after a few minutes. She sounded more normal. Less shaky.

"I'm not going to take advantage of you," Mara said, a bit of tease in her voice, but the world was coming back into focus. She had been so zeroed in on Kirby before. But now she was very aware that they were in a public bathroom in the Olympic Village.

"Mmm, no, please take advantage of me." Kirby's lips skimmed along Mara's jaw, and heat spread through Mara's body lightning fast.

"Hey," Mara whispered. "You don't have to—"

"I know I don't have to. Jesus." Kirby ripped herself away. She brushed her hair out of her face, frustration in every movement. She was still slightly unsteady, but her voice was strong.

"Don't do that." Anger rose in Mara, right along with desire. Was it always going to be that way with Kirby? Rage and longing in one shot.

"Do what?"

"Get mad at me for no reason."

"I don't do that," Kirby said.

"Yes, you do. And I do too. And it's ridiculous. The Olympics are in—"

"Stop lecturing me. I know when the Olympics start. I know I need to lock in, okay? What do you think I've been doing? You're not the only one in the world who cares, Mara May."

Mara was done. She grabbed a fistful of Kirby's shirt and pulled her forward.

"Fuck you," Mara whispered. Their lips didn't touch, but they were so, so close. She could feel Kirby's exhalations and smell whatever citrus-scented hair product she had in her waves.

"Don't talk dirty to me unless you want me to do something about it," Kirby said. A smile tipped her lips, and Mara found herself smiling too.

Kirby's gaze scanned over Mara's face. Usually, Mara would have hidden. Shuttered her emotions. Closed her eyes. She would have done whatever she needed to do to separate herself from that moment.

Compartmentalize.

But instead, she… didn't. She let Kirby look at her. She'd seen Kirby shaking and scared, so it was only fair.

"Let me kiss you," Kirby said, her voice almost too soft to hear.

Mara didn't respond, but she did lean in that last millimeter, closing the miniscule distance between them.

Their lips pressed together lightly. It was surprisingly sweet. By far the sweetest kiss they'd had. Mara's head spun as Kirby deepened the kiss, as her hands trailed over Mara's shoulders and throat.

"I'm scared of this," Kirby said, breaking the kiss way sooner than Mara was ready for.

Mara was breathless like she'd just finished a race. "You don't need to be."

Kirby shook her head. "You don't know… You don't know anything, Mara May."

"We should go," Mara whispered.

"Me first," Kirby said, and wasn't that amazing? So many double meanings in two little words. Kirby leaving first. Kirby placing first.

Kirby pulled away. Then she walked away. And Mara was left feeling like something had aligned rather than broken apart.

CHAPTER
FIFTEEN

MARA COULD SEE her wispy breaths in the cold night air. It was loud around her. Excited voices rising and falling. There were hugs and selfies and music blaring as Team USA waited for their entrance cue during the Parade of Nations in Milan.

It was a huge, raucous party. It hadn't been so *fun* last time she'd come to the Opening Ceremony. Mara lifted her face to the sky and let the overwhelming sound of athletes from so many countries wash over her. She felt unburdened, which was blatantly ridiculous. In reality, there was more pressure. More eyes on her. More expectations than ever before.

But she *felt* light.

She hadn't attended the Opening Ceremony at her last two Olympics, instead focusing on getting her head on straight in time for her first event. She didn't regret that now, but she knew she didn't want to miss the Opening Ceremony this time around.

Mara, Jordan, and Brandilyn had traveled to Milan with a few guys from the men's team, but other skiers, like Kirby, Lindsey, and Apollo had stayed in Val di Fiemme for the Predazzo Opening Ceremony events.

Mara was going to get pulled for an interview at any time. It had already been arranged with the major television network covering the Opening Ceremony, but she still had some time to take it all in.

Jordan grabbed her hand and before Mara knew it, Brandilyn's phone was in her face filming or taking pictures. She had no idea which. She smiled, and the rookies both grinned and posed in several different ways. The poses happened in such rapid succession that Mara froze. She was sure she looked the same in every photo. She really was old.

Brandilyn's cheeks were so rosy and her eyes so bright. And Jordan was talking so fast it was like someone had turned her voice on two-times speed. They were excited. And they had every reason to be. She had been terrified at her first Olympics. She couldn't remember smiling. It had been such serious business.

"There are so many hot guys here," Brandilyn whispered, and Mara laughed. She had been boy crazy at nineteen as well until she realized she wasn't actually that into boys.

"Hot girls too," Mara whispered back, nodding toward the women's hockey team who were taking pictures and dancing together, enjoying themselves. She mimed fanning herself.

Jordan and Brandilyn both reacted as if Mara had revealed an incredibly juicy secret about herself. And maybe she had. It wasn't something she talked about often, but the important people in her life knew.

And maybe Jordan and Brandilyn could be important to her.

Maybe Kirby could be too.

Jordan was bouncing up and down, asking her type, and pointing to every random woman around them, but Mara couldn't get a word in edgewise.

A hand touched her elbow, and Mara jumped. Out of habit, she shuttered all the happiness on her face as she turned toward a person with media credentials around their neck. And before she knew it, she was whisked over to the edge of the holding area so she could be interviewed for the Opening Ceremony broadcast.

She'd seen the interviewer, Ross McFadden, on TV during past Olympics, but she'd never met him.

"How are you feeling tonight, Mara?"

The impulse to lie was hovering right at the surface, but she could still see Jordan and Brandilyn in the crowd of athletes waiting to make their debut during the Parade of Nations. They were giggling about something. She could hear opera music, likely from the actual televised Opening Ceremony.

"I'm just..." She shook her head. "It's hard to explain, but I'm so, so happy. Tonight feels special. There's so much adrenaline and excitement," she said, words gushing out. "I'm so thankful I'm here."

He seemed taken aback by her response. Maybe he had expected her to be more somber. Precedent would have supported that expectation.

"This is your fourth Olympics. What makes this Opening Ceremony so special?"

"It's my last one." She hadn't planned to say that, but she couldn't imagine *not* saying it at that moment. Most people assumed, but she hadn't said so outright. "I'll compete in these Olympics and finish out the World Cup, and then I'm done. So maybe I'm looking at everything differently. Trying to see it through the eyes of someone who will never be back."

When she'd discussed it with her agent and, separately, her dad, they had agreed she should announce her retirement after winning her gold medal. The logic was that an announcement before the Olympics would be a distraction, but there was another reason. One that no one was admitting out loud.

If she waited until after the Olympics to announce her retirement, it gave her a chance to change her mind if she didn't win the gold. To try again and again. She could complete until she literally couldn't keep up anymore.

But she *would* win. She had to.

"So you're retiring after this World Cup season?"

"Yes. I'm ready. This just"—she gestured toward the huge group of athletes from the United States. She could see the delegations from Ukraine, United Arab Emirates, Uruguay, and Uzbekistan from where she was standing. There was such a sense of joy around her. "I want this to be my last one. It's beautiful here. And I'm having fun, and I'll be honest, the Olympics haven't always been fun for me. I want to have fun and move on on a high note. I see the fire in these young athletes coming up in cross-country skiing, and it's exciting. I'm ready to cheer them on."

"You mention not having fun in past Olympics. Is that a reference to losing the thirty-kilometer race four years ago? You were widely considered the front runner."

"It's not a reference to that." For once, she hadn't been thinking about that horrible race. "I put a lot of pressure on myself. I'm competitive. We all are. But it takes a toll." She thought back to Kirby's panic attack in the hallway. "It takes a toll on a lot of us. And it's important to do what's best for our own health. Mental and physical. What's best for me on all fronts is to *enjoy* my last Olympics. Enjoy myself for the rest of the World Cup. Then move on."

"I would like to ask you about your competitor and teammate, Kirby Bonham. She beat you in Beijing in the thirty-k mass start. She had never even hit the podium in that race, so it was a surprise for her to race so well. And—"

"Any high-level competitor can win a single race. All it takes is for someone to fall down or have a bad day or contract a cold or for the conditions to deteriorate. She won that day. I expect to win this time."

"You're saying her win was circumstantial?"

Mara laughed. She hadn't exactly meant it that way. It was wild how easily her words could be spun. But she liked the idea of Kirby seeing this interview and interpreting it that way. Maybe it would fire her up the same way Kirby's interviews emboldened Mara.

"I'm saying my record speaks for itself. And so does Kirby Bonham's."

"Is that shade?"

"Oh, I would never be shady," Mara said, mock disbelief in her voice. "Bonham is a great skier. She has more spirit than anyone I know. She's fearless. I underestimated her four years ago. I will not make that mistake again."

CHAPTER
SIXTEEN

KIRBY ZONED out in the athlete spectator area of the grandstand as music played and skiers made their way into the stadium for the skiathlon. The skiathlon was ten kilometers of classic style and ten of freestyle, with a transition to different gear halfway through.

Kirby hated racing the skiathlon, so she was happy to sit it out, but she felt anxious about it anyway.

She wanted Mara to do well. She shouldn't have cared. In past competitions, she hadn't rooted for Mara. She'd done the opposite.

But today, her body was vibrating with pre-race adrenaline, even though she was just standing around with a bunch of teammates.

She pulled out her phone and replayed a video she'd had cued up for a day.

Kirby had watched the clip of Mara's interview at the Opening Ceremony in Milan a hundred times. She looked gorgeous. Color high in her cheeks, her hair slightly frizzy for the first time in her life. She seemed almost intoxicated in the interview, riding high on the start of the Games.

Kirby wanted to fuck her. She wanted to kiss away the shade that had clearly been there. Ross McFadden had clocked it. Mara had insinuated that Kirby's win was due to a snowball of conditions and not Kirby's own grit and determination. It made Kirby angry and horny and fired up. And excited to race.

Mara had also called her fearless.

Even after seeing Kirby fight through a panic attack. Even after seeing the literal physical manifestation of fears and anxiety on Kirby's body, Mara had called her fearless.

It made Kirby *feel* fearless.

They would compete against each other only once. In their past Olympics together, they'd shared many starting lines, but for the Milan Cortina Olympics, Kirby had dropped the skiathlon and ten kilometer, and Mara had dropped all the sprints and team events.

So Kirby's only chances to shut Mara's beautiful mouth were in the press, in bed, or at the fifty-kilometer finish line.

And she wasn't going to wait the fifteen days for the fifty-k.

Apollo grabbed Kirby's hand as the skiers sidled up to the starting line, and Kirby put her phone away. She needed to stop obsessing over Mara saying, *"My record speaks for itself. And so does Kirby Bonham's,"* in a way that made Kirby want to pin her to a wall and make her take it back.

Apollo had a sign that said *Go Lindsey* in huge block letters. He seemed nervous. The skiathlon was Lindsey's best event.

No one had a *Go Mara* sign, which wasn't a shock, but still made Kirby feel bad.

Mara looked good, though. Focused. She had on new purple sunglasses. Not the silver ones she always wore at practice and that Kirby had placed on her head after the first time they'd had sex.

The race opened with a bang and the skiers shot off the starting line. It was a decent start for Mara. For Lindsey too. Before Kirby had fully taken it all in, Mara was out of sight, but there were huge screens broadcasting the racers as they made their way along the course.

Mara was a beautiful skier. The push and power in her body was effortless, every movement practiced and optimized to propel her forward. She'd never really *watched* Mara ski. She had spent most of her adult life skiing with Mara, against her. Usually chasing her. But she had never taken herself out of the equation.

Mara was incredible. She was so in control of every movement in her body. So aware of the field of skiers.

It was the opposite of their hookups where she gave up all that control to Kirby.

"When did you get back from Milan?" Apollo asked Jordan, leaning around Kirby to see her. Jordan had traveled to Milan with Mara. Kirby had to shake herself out of her thoughts.

"This morning. Mara came back late last night. Can you believe she announced her retirement? She's been living on the podium lately. Why retire now?"

"She wants to go out on a high note," Kirby said. She couldn't look away from the screen as a huge cluster of skiers rounded a bend. Mara was in the front pack with Lindsey hanging in the middle.

"But what if it's like last time?" Jordan said. "She choked."

Kirby glanced at Jordan sharply. "She won a silver medal. That's hardly a choke."

"Oh. I just mean. I don't know. Everyone said she was going to win the thirty kilometer. They'd practically chiseled her name on the gold before the race even started."

"Yeah, pretty asinine, huh?" Kirby said wryly. She had always been salty about it, but less so now. Mara deserved to race without the weight of the world's expectations on her.

The skiers were making the transition from classic to freestyle. Lindsey made a strategic push and jumped into third while Mara fell back slightly. She would probably be able to gain it back, but it was not an insignificant delay.

Suddenly, Kirby's breath caught, and she took an involuntary step toward the screen. Her body moved before her brain caught up.

A skier from the Netherlands lost control behind Mara. It caused a chain reaction. The skier flailed before regaining control, but in the unsteadiness, her ski clipped Mara's, causing her to spin out.

The whole stadium jumped to their feet and gasped—a full two seconds after Kirby had done so.

Time seemed to slow as Mara went down.

Careers had been ended by crashes.

Kirby felt a wave of nausea as a skier from Japan had to

swerve to avoid her. Then one from Canada. Both were able to keep their feet and continue racing.

It happened so fast, and before Kirby could freak out about Mara being hurt, Mara had popped up. Her momentum was lost, starting from zero with diminished energy. But she surged forward, digging deep.

Everything in Kirby's body ached for what had happened. Every skier had faced something similar at some point in their career, but for it to happen at the Olympics was terrible.

She watched Mara push and push to catch back up with the middle of the pack, but it was too big a setback.

A hand slipped into hers and tugged. It was Apollo. She looked around wildly and realized she was the only one still staring at the big screen with her heart in her throat.

She knew the cameras were on them. The networks loved to show Team USA cheering in the stands.

So had they caught that? Had they seen Kirby heartbroken for Mara as everyone else moved on to cheering for Lindsey and other skiers?

Kirby's stomach hurt as the leaders came back into the stadium. A roar went up in the crowd. A young skier from Italy was in the front, and Kirby had never heard such a celebration from a cross-country skiing stadium.

Lindsey was in fifth, but she had momentum on the skiers in front of her. Apollo screamed his head off and lifted his sign. Kirby was shocked he had hidden his feelings for Lindsey for five years. They seemed very, very on display at the moment.

Even more than hers had.

Lindsey gained and passed the skier in front of her, moving into fourth. Then in a burst, she pushed into third.

Kirby started screaming then too. Lindsey was a veteran. This was her second Olympics, but she hadn't come close to medaling four years ago.

Right before the finish line, Lindsey leveled up with the second-place skier. In a blur of motion, both skiers lunged across the finish line, a skill they all practiced over and over again to get their boot over the line first. But Kirby had no idea who had placed second and who had placed third just from watching the screen.

Lindsey and the skier from Finland both collapsed in the snow after crossing the finish line. As the results popped up on the board, Lindsey covered her face with her hands in shock.

"Oh my God," Apollo whispered. "I think I'm in love with a silver medalist."

Kirby laughed, charmed by her best friend.

Soon, Mara crossed the finish line too. She didn't collapse like so many other racers. She rarely did. The stoic, breathe-through-the-pain princess. Never show vulnerability. Never show anything. She was gasping, though, a small grimace with every inhale and exhale, her chest heaving. Kirby felt for her so viscerally. To have to build back momentum from a dead stop took a massive physiological toll. After Mara recovered, she and the skier from the Netherlands chatted.

There were lots of cameras pointed in their direction, and Kirby hated that for her. Mara didn't revel in the limelight. Kirby wanted to take that attention away from her but not for the usual reasons. Not because Kirby naturally wanted attention. No, she just sought to shield Mara from the eyes of the world.

But then Mara smiled—it was the real smile that Kirby coveted but rarely received—and hugged the other woman.

It was a shocking reaction. Kirby hadn't expected Mara to punch anyone, but she also hadn't expected warmth. And there was no doubt that interaction had been warm.

From there, Mara found Lindsey and saw she'd won silver. Then they were hugging too.

"Think she'll hug you when you beat her in the fifty kilometer?" Apollo asked.

"No. Definitely not."

IT WAS LATE. Too late to be making her way to Kirby's door, but Mara couldn't sleep.

She'd forgotten what it was like after a race at the Olympics. The press in the exchange zone. The hoops to jump through.

All Mara wanted to do was hide.

No, that wasn't quite true. All Mara wanted was to hide in Kirby's bed.

Not the best impulse in the middle of the most important competition of her life.

But, still, she knocked.

Their hallway had American flag pennant banners taped from wall to wall. She'd seen the ski jumpers decorating yesterday. Kirby's door had a picture of the Statue of Liberty on it.

Lady Liberty swung inward as Jordan answered. Because of course Jordan answered.

"Oh, Mara!" Then Jordan was hugging her, which was

about the nicest thing in the entire world. "I'm so sorry. Are you okay?"

Over Jordan's shoulder, Mara saw Kirby sit up in bed.

"I'm fine. Can't sleep."

It was five days until Mara competed again. She needed to put the skiathlon behind her, but she deserved one night to wallow. Right?

It was only three days until Kirby's first event. The sprint classic.

She should have been letting Kirby rest. Letting Kirby focus.

"You should come in. We can watch a movie or gossip. Kirby and I were looking at the options on Hinge," Jordan said. Sweet, young Jordan. She had a few star-shaped, acne-healing stickers on her face—a trend that, again, made Mara feel very old.

"Hinge." Mara felt like her brain was buried under snow.

"It's a dating app," Jordan said.

"I know." It shouldn't have been a surprise that Kirby was looking at a dating app. And it didn't mean anything. Mara logically knew it didn't mean anything.

Just like she logically knew that their occasional collisions resulting in orgasms also didn't mean anything.

Kirby got out of bed. She was in boxers and that black sports bra Mara was becoming obsessed with. She pulled on a pair of sweats.

Mara had made a mistake. There was no way to get out of this situation without setting off Jordan's alarm bells. Jordan might have been young, but she wasn't oblivious. She would realize something weird was going on.

"I promised Kirby I'd film a TikTok with her," Mara stuttered out. Every other cross-country skier on the team, men and women, had appeared in one of Kirby's videos by that point. She posted one every day, filling her feed with constant Olympic content. Mara hadn't posted once since getting to Italy.

"Oh." Jordan glanced at Kirby, a bit bewildered. "That's cool. Should I leave?"

"Of course not," Kirby said. They were the first words she'd uttered, and it was a shot straight through Mara's stomach. "We can go to the lounge. You need to go to sleep, Jordan. Your training time is bright and early."

"Yes, Mom," Jordan said with a smiling eyeroll.

Mara felt a rush of tenderness toward her young teammate, and she impulsively gave Jordan another hug. "Thank you. We'll look at Hinge together some other time."

Kirby ushered Jordan back into their room, grabbed one of the welcome gift bags they'd all received off a table by the door, and led Mara down the hallway.

"Do you even have Hinge?" Kirby asked, her voice clipped.

"No, but I've heard I can get it on this fancy thing I own called a phone."

"Jesus Christ, you're being very weird."

Mara shrugged, feeling lost. "I just need some anger management."

Kirby pinned Mara to a wall so quickly, it was like Mara had been transported.

"Anyone could see us here," Mara managed, but she almost didn't care. She ran her fingertips down the ditch of Kirby's spine, and Kirby shuddered.

Then Kirby ripped herself away.

"Lindsey isn't in my room."

"Where is she? Doing press?" Kirby asked.

"No. I think she's…" Mara didn't want to say. She had suspicions, but she didn't want to give away a secret that wasn't hers to tell.

"Oh, she's with Apollo?" Kirby said.

Evidently that was a bit more common knowledge than Mara had suspected.

"That's my guess."

Kirby grabbed Mara's hand and pulled her down the hallway.

"I wonder where Apollo's roommate is," Kirby said.

"We're all playing musical beds. Someone is going to be without a place to sleep. Not that I'm expecting you to sleep with me. If you don't want to. I know that's not what this—"

"Mara, shut up." Kirby grabbed the key from Mara and yanked open her door.

Mara expected to be shoved onto the bed, but Kirby just stared at her once the door shut behind them.

"It's okay to be sad," Kirby whispered.

Mara nodded. She was sad. But it still didn't quite feel real. Soon, it would catch up with her, but it hadn't yet.

She'd hugged her mom, who she hadn't seen in months, after the race. Then her dad, who had been tightlipped but kind enough. She'd thrown away her new sunglasses.

Because she was sure that would make her feel better. It hadn't. Then she'd turned off her phone and drifted through the rest of the day in a daze.

Until right then, when the world sharpened into focus on Kirby's lips, her mouth, her smile.

Kirby cupped Mara's chin and tilted her head back, so Mara was forced to meet her eyes.

"Let me take care of you."

She already was. "Okay."

Kirby helped Mara undress. She tugged Mara's shirt over her head. Her hair fell in a mess over her shoulders and down her back. Her bra came off next, followed by her sweats and panties.

Was it the first time she'd been totally naked with Kirby? It felt like it.

"You too," Mara murmured as she half-heartedly shoved at the waistband of Kirby's sweatpants.

Kirby flung the pants off, then the rest of her clothes too.

They lay together looking their fills, like two virgins who had never done it before. Mara discovered more tattoos on Kirby's body—a moth on her shoulder blade, tiny snowflakes falling down her ribs. And Kirby rubbed her back in long sweeps until Mara was practically wrapped around her in her desire to get closer. To feel Kirby's hands.

Mara felt like she had to say something important, something urgent, as her fingertips explored the bumps of Kirby's rib cage, the soft flesh of her ass, the strong stretch of muscle down her thigh.

"You didn't kiss me the last time we did this. And I

didn't kiss you," was what slipped out when Mara opened her mouth. That had haunted Mara, that she hadn't taken full advantage. Every time could be their last, and she needed to treat it that way.

"We kissed in the bathroom. After my panic attack."

"That was a good kiss," Mara said.

"It was. Top-of-the-podium kissing."

Mara started to smile, but Kirby pressed their lips together before her smile fully formed. Gently, and then harder as Mara's body pushed for more.

Kirby rolled Mara onto her back. Mara spread her thighs and wrapped her legs around Kirby's.

"Mmm, one day, I'll fuck you like this," Kirby said, her voice slow and sleepy. "Get a nice big strap-on and fill you up."

Mara arched at the words. She didn't know if *one day* would be possible, but it turned her on anyway.

"Kirby," Mara whispered. The name tasted sweet on her lips. In her mouth.

"I've got you, princess."

They kissed again. Syrupy slow. And Kirby slipped her fingers into Mara. Their bodies moved together. It felt dreamlike. Almost like Mara was half asleep. Her muscles hurt, from the race and from the fall. But every clench felt unbelievable.

"I'm gonna come," Mara said, dazed at how a few fingers were about to shatter her so easily.

Kirby brushed their lips together, and Mara's breath went haywire. Kirby kissed her deeper, her lush lips more overwhelming than her fingers.

A surge of pleasure flooded through Mara. And another, cresting slow, slow, slowly. She gasped at the end, having to rip her mouth away. Kirby kept kissing her.

Her neck, her jaw, her ear.

"I should lose more often," Mara whispered.

Kirby laughed against her skin. "If you let me do this every time you lose, I'll have to agree."

"Your turn," Mara said. She went to sit up. To do *something* to make Kirby feel good. Anything.

"No, it's okay. Take a minute to recover, Mara. We have time."

But they *didn't* have time. Their whole life was a race. Three days to Kirby's next event. Five to Mara's. Fifteen to the fifty-k. It felt like forever and also not nearly enough time.

Plus, Lindsey could open that door at any second, and that was a risk they both should have been worried about.

But Mara *was* exhausted. Every reserve of energy in her body had been expended during the skiathlon. Which she'd lost spectacularly.

Mara didn't want to face that.

"Will you just talk? Distract me, but I don't... I don't know."

"You don't want to talk back?"

"I want to listen to you."

Kirby cupped her cheek, and they stared at each other.

It was too much. Mara closed her eyes, blocking everything out except Kirby's skin against hers. And Kirby's voice as she started talking.

She talked about skiing gossip, and random reality stars

she knew, and the things she'd seen in the stands that day. Lots of things Mara didn't give a crap about. And Mara let Kirby's voice wash over her until her aching muscles relaxed, and she fell asleep.

She wasn't sure how long she'd been out, but when the room came back into focus, Kirby was humming off-key and braiding small sections of Mara's hair.

Mara tried not to move because she didn't want Kirby to stop, but Kirby seemed to be a thousand miles away. She had earphones in. Her mouth was soft. She looked younger. Innocent.

When Kirby noticed Mara was awake, she put her earphones away.

"What were you listening to?" Mara asked.

"Sad girl pop."

"Don't be sad." Mara kissed her chin. Kirby's arms tightened, and a hand delved deep into Mara's hair, tipping her head back.

Mara's body zipped fully awake, and she moaned. Kirby glanced at her, surprise clear on her face.

"What?" Mara asked.

"That's the loudest sound I've heard you make."

"Oh."

"You like it when I pull your hair."

During any of their other times together, Mara would have rolled her eyes or said *duh*. But her brain felt too fuzzy to play. To fight.

"Do you like it rough, Mara May?" Kirby asked. It sounded as much like a genuine question as it did dirty talk.

"When you do it, yes," she said. Which was way, way too revealing.

Mara and Kirby had done this a few times now, and it was always a blur and a rush. Kirby was more than generous, and Mara was a greedy little monster.

"I want to make you come," Mara said.

Kirby studied her for a long moment. "Then lie on your back."

Kirby fanned Mara's hair out on the twin bed before leaning in to kiss her.

"Your mouth. It's unfair how much I think about it," Kirby admitted. "Those lips. Fuck."

Then, without fanfare or warning, Kirby threw her leg over Mara and straddled her face. Her knees were on the ends of Mara's hair, tugging it, stinging her scalp, and holding her down.

Mara's hands grabbed Kirby's ass, fingertips digging in. "Oh, God. I've never done this. Like this, I mean."

"Do you want to?" Kirby asked.

"Yes."

"Good." Kirby dragged her pussy over Mara's lips. She was wet. And she tasted incredible.

"Fuck," Mara whispered. It was hard to get the angle right with Kirby on her hair, but it also made her feel a bit wild. Like it truly was a fight. A fight and an exposure all in one.

Kirby twitched her hips and planted a hand on the wall. Mara wished she could step outside of herself to watch Kirby work her magic, to see her, head thrown back, hips rocking, fully naked.

"Your mouth is so sweet, princess," Kirby panted.

Mara let her fingers play through the wetness between Kirby's legs. She couldn't get her fingers as deep as she wanted, but that simple touch made Kirby groan.

This position felt very vulnerable. Submissive.

Kirby was fucking against her face, dragging her clit over Mara's tongue, her lips. Her pussy drenched Mara's chin.

And Mara's mind went blissfully blank, and not in the way she forced it to when she was scared or shy or upset. Not compartmentalization to protect herself.

No, this was freedom. And she wanted it to last forever.

But it didn't.

Kirby reached down and fisted Mara's hair. Then she froze, arched, and shuddered again and again.

And that was pretty mind-blowing too. Feeling Kirby lose it. Hearing her shout, even though they should not have been shouting in the middle of the Olympic Village.

"Holy shit," Kirby rasped out, ripples flowing through her. She fell next to Mara on the bed. "You're trouble, Mara May."

"The good kind, I hope."

"Eh," Kirby closed her eyes. She had sweat on her shoulders and throat. Her cheeks were red. She was the sexiest person Mara had ever seen. "Verdict's still out."

CHAPTER
EIGHTEEN

KIRBY SET up her phone to record her and Mara. They'd moved to the abandoned lounge so as to not be caught in flagrante by Lindsey. The space was usually full of athletes watching events on TV, but it was a ghost town in the middle of the night.

Kirby normally had ring lights and all kinds of shit to make everyone appear gorgeous and clear on camera, but Mara didn't need help looking gorgeous.

She'd put on a tight, baby-pink, athletic tank top that zipped up the front and a matching pair of wide leg yoga pants, like a trendy Pilates influencer. Kirby longed to lower the zipper between Mara's tits with her teeth.

Kirby was still in her sports bra and sweats. They both looked a little sex bedraggled, and that thrilled Kirby.

"First things first," Kirby said after hitting record. "Mara, have you gone through your welcome bag yet?"

"No." Mara was sitting up very straight, stiff as a board.

"Great. Guess how many condoms are in here."

Kirby had refused to tell her the video topic, and Mara had agreed with less fight than Kirby had expected.

"Really? That's what we're doing? We're talking about condoms?" Mara said, plainly unimpressed.

"Yes. We're doing an unboxing." Kirby chucked a bunch of stuff out of the bag. Some lotions. A sleep mask. A bracelet. Chocolate.

"Hey, I'd take that."

Kirby tossed the candy to her, and Mara opened it and popped it into her mouth. Kirby forced her gaze away from Mara's lips.

"Okay, how many condoms?" Kirby repeated.

"I don't know. Twelve," she said offhandedly.

"Twelve! Geez, who is going through that many condoms through the course of the Games?"

"That's less than one a day, KB." Mara lifted her nose, all snooty, and Kirby wanted to pin her to the lounge sofa.

Mara had called her KB, like their other teammates. But it sounded so mean when Mara said it. Kirby loved it.

"Well, we can all hope to be as ambitious as Mara May."

Mara gave her the clearest, dirtiest look, and Kirby knew this video was going to be gold.

She pulled a skinny box out of the bag. It was fancy for a sleeve of condoms.

"Mmm, nice box," Kirby said.

Mara threw her head back and laughed, a true, loud laugh, and Kirby realized her mistaken euphemism.

Then she did pin Mara to the sofa, kissing the hell out of her. Her hand tangled in Mara's hair, and Mara went under so easily it made Kirby's head spin. They kissed for one long minute. Then another.

Kirby forced herself away.

"You can't show that," Mara gasped out.

"I know." Kirby fixed Mara's hair, taking longer than necessary because she just wanted to touch. "I'll cut it out."

Once they'd both stopped breathing hard, Kirby lifted the first condom out of the box. It had a pink wrapper with a cartoon animal on it.

"What is this?" Kirby said. "A rat?"

"It's the Olympic mascot. She's a stoat."

"A stoat? It's adorable you know that."

"It's adorable they put her on a condom," Mara said. "Nothing says passion like a cartoon weasel. Let me do the next one." She lifted one out of the box. "Oh, it's a dental dam."

"Sweet." Kirby plucked it out of Mara's hand, playfully slipped it into her pocket, and winked at the camera.

Mara rolled her eyes.

The next condoms they pulled out were colored to look like gold, silver, and bronze medals.

"So you can make the podium, even if you don't make the podium," Mara said, deadpan, and Kirby laughed.

She was impressed with how well Mara was doing. She'd even made a joke.

Kirby held up the gold one. "If you can't get an actual gold medalist inside you, this is the next best thing."

Mara giggled, which set Kirby off too. She would have to cut some of the laughing, but she wanted that smile on Mara's face to last forever.

They finished going through the box of condoms and dental dams. Mara was a great sport but also played up their animosity enough to be believable. She acted very put-upon, especially by the time they'd seen their third condom with the Olympic mascot on it.

There *were* twelve condoms total—a mix between male and female—plus dental dams.

"All right, Mara," Kirby said, wrapping it up. "And what do you think about the selection of safe-sex accoutrements provided to us?"

"I don't know. It's good for athletes who have the time for stuff like that."

"Oh, and Princess Mara is too busy to think about something as pedestrian as sex?"

Mara gave her the most hateful glare, which sent Kirby's brain and body in two opposite directions. Kirby's body had learned that Mara's contempt often led to the hottest sex ever. But Kirby's brain was worried she'd gone one step too far.

"You can fuck all you want. Wear yourself out for the fifty-k, Bonham."

"Oh, I will," Kirby laughed. "I'll cut it there."

Mara stood up. "I didn't like that."

Kirby stood too. "Me calling you Princess Mara, or—"

"*Or.*" Mara shook out her arms like she was trying to fling something gross off her body. "But also you calling me Princess Mara. I don't love that."

"Sometimes you do love it, though," Kirby said. Mara definitely loved it when she was naked and about to come.

"Everyone is going to think I'm such a prude. Obviously, I have time for sex. We just had sex. But I *should* be too busy for sex. We both should be resting. I should be asleep. You should be getting your head together. God, Kirby, you have the sprint in two days."

That sounded so responsible. And innocuous. But Kirby bristled at Mara's roundabout reference to getting her head on straight. She probably hadn't meant it in relation to Kirby's panic attacks, but that was where Kirby's mind went. Because anxiety about her anxiety was always right there on the surface. She tried to pull out the mantra that occasionally helped calm her, helped her feel less upset—*it is okay to feel out of control*—but it wasn't hitting right. She didn't like losing control of this moment at all.

"You worry about yourself, Mara. I've been multi-tasking my whole life. I can handle a little booty call every once in a while and still perform. Trust me. This is nothing."

Mara stopped her fidgeting and went motionless. "*Nothing.*" Mara nodded. "Okay. Good. I agree."

Silence descended between them, and it felt like the old Mara—the Mara that had iced Kirby out for years, the pre-Janette Collins interview Mara—was in the lounge instead of the angry, passionate woman Kirby had become obsessed with.

Kirby didn't know how to get them back to the hot and fun place they'd been not five minutes prior. She stood, crowding Mara. Mara's breath sped up. Kirby wrapped her fingers around the wild tendrils of Mara's hair that fell over her shoulder, and Mara's eyes fluttered closed.

There. Perfect.

Kirby took a step back, and Mara swayed.

"I'll walk you back to your room. You're exhausted," Kirby said.

Kirby didn't touch Mara on the walk, but she wanted to.

They reached Mara's door. Someone, surely *not* Mara, had taped a huge red, white, and blue smiley face poster on it. Kirby wasn't patriotic. She didn't go for the rah-rah America stuff. But the decoration was so silly and whimsical, it made her smile.

"I want to kiss you again," Kirby admitted as Mara's hand went to the door handle.

Mara's lips tipped up at one end, not a full smile but almost. "Yeah. I want that too."

Then Mara opened her door and went inside. It closed behind her, leaving Kirby staring at the poster. She pressed her forehead to the smiley face's forehead and laughed. There wasn't anything else she could do.

NINETEEN

THERE WAS icy fog in the morning air, making the starting line moody and dramatic. Kirby had slept poorly and woken up early, too agitated to sleep any longer. She'd spent all morning slowly warming up her muscles and fueling for the classic sprint events.

In Kirby's experience, it was impossible to be fully prepared for the Olympics. She had come to her first Olympic Games when she was twenty-four. At that point, she'd only been skiing competitively for a few years. She'd gotten to race a sprint heat after the flu had taken a teammate down. Kirby had been so naïve. So new to the sport. Naturally gifted but inexperienced.

It had felt so extraordinary. The excitement in the air. The pomp. The optimistic sportsmanship.

Every time she'd hit an Olympic course since, that anticipation and hope rushed up on her like a sense memory. It didn't matter that she was a gold medalist now and not the young adult who had come last in her very first Olympic heat. It didn't matter that she was a pseudo-celebrity and not a relative unknown entity.

The Olympics were always special and beautiful and so fucking stressful.

If everything went well, she would race four times in the next four hours, from qualification, quarterfinals, semifinals, to finals.

Coach Wu approached her in the warm-up area. She glanced around thoughtfully. *"One misty moisty morning, when cloudy was the weather…"*

Kirby stared at her blankly.

"Not a nursery rhyme fan?" Coach Wu said, humor in her voice. "That one's my favorite. There's leather."

"I'll be honest, Coach. I'm not going to be much for banter today, I don't think."

Coach Wu smiled. "That's a first. You looked good in warm-ups. Do you feel good?"

Kirby considered the question. It came down to appearance versus reality. Her outward presentation versus the turmoil in her head and heart. Looking good versus feeling good.

Seeing Mara crash during the skiathlon. Taking care of her afterward. Filming together. It was too much. Too many emotional swings, and she'd begun to worry the chaos would trigger a panic attack. The attacks loomed over her like a guillotine threatening to fall without warning. She'd finally spoken to one of the sports psychologists who had traveled with Team USA, and she'd done a videocall with a therapist as well. They weren't magicians who could cure her over the course of an hour, but she felt more settled.

And she'd realized she needed a breath to get through her first race before jumping headlong into another battle with Mara. Whatever form that battle might take.

It was okay to feel out of control.

But it was also okay to take back control when possible.

"Actually, yes. I do feel good."

"Head is where it should be?"

Kirby nodded. Coach Wu had been checking in consistently over the past week without being pushy. Both were appreciated. The checking in and the giving space.

"Go make them regret underestimating you, KB." Coach Wu gave her a trademark shoulder pat before Kirby made her way to the starting line to begin the qualification round where the thirty fastest skiers would move to the quarter-final heats.

Her heart was hammering in her ears. She took a breath, filling her lungs with frosty air. Then another. Then suddenly crystal clarity flushed through her. It was a sensation she was always chasing but rarely caught. The stillness. The way time slowed, and her thoughts quieted, and the only thing that existed was the snow in front of her, the tension in her muscles as she waited to explode off the starting line, and the silence as she waited for her signal.

And *bang*.

She was off.

The sprint course at Tesero Stadium was exactly her kind of course. It was fast with a hard climb up a hill before a long straightaway to the finish line.

She pushed for the whole race, but there was strategy

involved. She needed to qualify but also preserve energy for the later heats.

When the finish line came into view, she saw the Olympic rings imposed on the course and clocked the cheers from the crowd for the first time. She zipped through the finish line and slid to a stop.

She smiled and waved a pole at the crowd before putting her hands on her hips to try to breathe through the pain of exertion.

Her time was fine. She was solidly within the top fifteen and would easily move to the quarterfinal heats.

She glanced toward the athlete cheering section where she'd watched Mara and Lindsey race the skiathlon. She couldn't make out individuals, but it was full.

Was Mara watching her race today? Or was she resting and preparing herself for her next event? That would have been the responsible thing for Mara to do, and Mara was responsible.

But Kirby was going to medal today. She could feel it. She was hungry for it. And most importantly, she wanted to do it in front of Mara. She wanted Mara to see her make the podium.

Would Mara be happy for her? Or jealous? Frustrated?

Who could say? But Kirby wanted her to feel something, *anything*, about it.

The qualification race ended, and Kirby searched through the results board for her fellow teammates.

Jordan had placed twenty-fifth, so she would move on to the quarterfinal heats. Brandilyn's time had put her at thirty-first.

Kirby's stomach dropped. To be so close and miss out was devastating. Brandilyn had been expected to easily qualify. She found Jordan and Brandilyn in a hoard of skiers being shuffled around. They were hugging. Brandilyn was laughing but had tears on her cheeks.

"I'm fine. I'm fine," Brandilyn said as Kirby wrapped them in a big joint hug. "I fucked up and bobbled a turn. I'm fine."

But it wasn't fine. Brandilyn was young. She had such a huge career ahead of her. She would hopefully have many more chances at racing in the Olympics, but the sprint was her best event. It had to be shattering.

That was a trademark of the Olympics, though. High highs. Low lows.

Coach Wu moved Jordan and Kirby toward their area with stationary bikes to keep their muscles warm and physiological state primed until the quarterfinal heats, and a handler ushered Brandilyn over to her parents. Brandilyn was limping a little. As her parents enveloped her, Brandilyn really started to cry.

And Kirby felt like crying too. What a terrible, wonderful, terrible thing they put themselves through. For it all to come down to slightly less than three minutes of racing, a few tenths of a second, and 1585 meters.

Mara had shown up. She'd watched Kirby's qualification round. Then the quarterfinal.

Kirby had come first in her quarterfinal heat. Jordan had

come in third in her heat but had snagged one of the lucky loser qualifying spots by having the best time among skiers who didn't place first or second.

Rumors had started to pop through their phones and gossip channels about an injury, but Mara tried not to speculate. Brandilyn would be okay. She had to be. Mara was superstitious about injuries. She pretended like it was an impossibility to be taken out by one.

The men's quarterfinal heats took place after the women's and Apollo got second in his, so he was moving on to the semifinals. It was a bit of an upset. The exhilaration and noise from the athlete spectator zone was insane.

As Kirby lined up for her semifinal heat, the tension in the crowd ratcheted up. Kirby shook out her arms and adjusted her sunglasses. They were the black ones Mara had bought for her. They'd never talked about it. Kirby had never mentioned it.

Mara's heart rocketed into her throat. She felt sick. She wanted Kirby to do well. She cared.

She really, really cared.

And in the past, she hadn't. Or, maybe, more truthfully, she had hoped Kirby wouldn't succeed. She had wished poor times and upsets on Kirby as punishment for that thirty-k mess four years ago. It wasn't very nice, but it was her truth.

Now, it was terrifying to care so much about an event she wasn't even freaking racing. She didn't like it.

Mara was frozen with her eyes on the large screen showing the skiers sprint up the hill, arms pumping. She willed Kirby to go faster. Faster.

She wasn't going to make it. She wasn't going to qualify for the finals.

Lindsey was next to her, even-keeled as always.

"I don't think I can watch this," Mara whispered. She almost never came to races that weren't her own. There were too many emotions as a spectator. It screwed with her calm. She needed zen.

"It'll be close," Lindsey said, focused on the screen as Kirby powered into the stadium in third.

"I'm going to go."

Lindsey glanced at her sharply. "What?"

But Mara was already making her way through the crowd. She hurried to the exit. Heard the cheers as skiers crossed the finish line, but she couldn't bring herself to look at the results board.

Mara had gone to a Super Bowl party once in high school. She remembered her friend's mom being so into one of the teams that she couldn't even watch the game. She had paced between the kitchen and her bedroom, occasionally peeking at the TV to see the score. Mara had asked her why she wasn't watching if she cared so much.

She'd responded that it was too stressful. Every play felt like torture.

That was how Mara felt right then. It was torture watching Kirby ski.

Mara had been clocking incremental changes she would have made if it had been her racing. Monday morning quarterbacking. And her heart was pounding harder than when she competed, her whole body going haywire with anticipatory excitement and stress.

People said hi to Mara as she left the stadium. Someone asked Mara where she was going, but she didn't respond.

Then suddenly she was free and relatively alone. She took a shuttle back to the Olympic Village.

On the ride, she closed her eyes and tried to breathe through the turmoil in her body. She wanted to check her phone. By now, Apollo would have raced in his semifinal heat, and she felt bad for not being there to cheer him on. Which was ridiculous. She had never even had a conversation with him that didn't involve topics like the weather or protein powder.

When she got to the Olympic Village, rather than putzing around her room or pulling up the results of Kirby's race, she went to the gym and did as much weight training as she could without overextending herself. Then she ate dinner alone. And finally, hours after leaving the Tesero Stadium, she felt calm.

Worrying about Kirby shouldn't have affected her like that. It was a distraction, one that had wasted a whole day when she should have been preparing. It was scary.

She needed to get a grip. She had a race in two days. The interval start freestyle ten-k. She had a bronze medal in that event from Pyeongchang. That was what she should have been focusing on. Rather than letting herself get worked up over Kirby Bonham.

Two days to the ten-k. Twelve to the fifty.

Lindsey was in their room reading a paperback when Mara returned.

"Hey!" Lindsey said, sitting up in bed. "Are you sick or something? I was worried about you."

"No. I'm fine."

"So you rushed off because *why*? You don't give a shit about Kirby, Jordan, or Apollo?"

The accusation surprised her. Not because the perception of her was a surprise. She knew her teammates grinded against her status as the top skier in their sport. Her persona as a sweetheart and team leader versus the reality of her personality.

But it was a surprise coming from Lindsey.

"No. I do."

"Apollo made the finals. And you weren't there to cheer him on."

"Did he medal?" Mara asked.

The glare Lindsey gave her could have melted a medal. "That's not the only important thing in the world, Mara."

"Right. How did, uh, Jordan and Kirby do?"

She really only wanted to know about Kirby but admitting that was too revealing.

"Look it up yourself." Lindsey shook her head and went back to her book. It was a murder mystery with a cat and lots of baked goods on the cover.

Mara stood there awkwardly. She felt like she shouldn't stay there, but it was her room. She had nowhere else to go. She felt kind of sick again. Like she'd just wrecked something very important.

CHAPTER
TWENTY

KIRBY MADE her way to the exchange zone where the press was waiting after the sprint final. She was buzzing.

There was an Olympic doping officer following her, waiting to collect a drug testing sample. That was a fun little novelty she'd forgotten about since her medals in Beijing. They would take a sample as soon as she made it through the exchange zone and back inside the Tesero facility.

She walked down the line of press. In Beijing, there had been a complicated dance of microphones, masking, and social distancing because of Covid. But now it was a free-for-all.

"Kirby Bonham! Kirby Bonham!" reporters yelled to get her attention.

She spotted a journalist named Henrik Jensen. "Hi, Henrik."

He was a reporter for a popular online winter sports

magazine. She'd done an interview with him once in Park City.

"Congratulations," he said. "How do you feel about the results of the sprint?"

"Great! After almost missing out on the final heat altogether, I couldn't be happier about a bronze medal. I haven't hit the podium in that event in a few years, so it's very exciting."

"Your teammates were there cheering you on after your race. It seems like there is a lot of camaraderie in this group of skiers," Henrik said.

It was a leading comment. Everyone knew the team got along, but not her and Mara. He was clearly guiding her in that direction.

But she didn't mind being led occasionally.

"Not all of my teammates, but most of them, yes," Kirby said with a smile. Mara had been absent. Which Kirby had expected, but it still stung. "It's a special team. Lots of young and hungry skiers."

Jordan and Brandilyn were so talented, and they would only get better. As long as Brandilyn's injury wasn't career ending, but Kirby wasn't letting her mind go there. The men's team had a ton of rookies and first-time Olympians too. Skiers like her, Lindsey, Apollo, and Mara were the millennials whose days were numbered.

Which was why Kirby had worked so hard at the Hollywood stuff. She wasn't going to be able to ski competitively forever.

"This is the first time in the Olympics you haven't raced

the sprint against Mara May. Did you miss competing against her?"

"Of course. Mara is the best, and it's a lot more fun defeating the best. *I would know.* But I'll get my chance soon. I'll get her in the fifty kilometer."

There. That had been nice. And also not so nice.

Maybe it would send Mara running back to Kirby in a fit. A girl could dream.

She hadn't spoken to Mara since the night after the skiathlon. Kirby wasn't avoiding her, but she wasn't seeking her out either. And Mara seemed to be on the same page.

Mara hadn't even been there to watch the finals.

"There are rumors there has been conflict between you during training," Henrik Jensen said.

"Oh? Me and conflict? Never!" Kirby said, putting her hand to her chest. She assumed teasers of their Janette Collins interview were starting to air. Not that that was the only proof of their animosity. The proof was prolific at this point. Their condom unboxing video had exploded online. Mara's sexual repression had read as seething dislike on camera. "I'm a little sweetie. I would never cause conflict."

Henrik smiled, but she could tell he wasn't going to be satisfied with a little sarcasm.

"You're known for making tactical, sharp, strategic moves. You're not conservative."

"No. I'm not. In *any* arena of my life."

"But Mara is a conservative skier. She doesn't take strategic risks like you."

Kirby was aggravated he kept returning to that well. She'd won a medal. Not Mara. And anyway, Mara didn't often need to take risks. She made the podium just fine without doing so.

"Mara doesn't matter. I'm racing the relay in four days. The team sprint in six. She's opted out of competing with me in either, which was the right thing for her. I'm putting my focus toward those races. I'll take care of Mara after that."

Kirby moved on, answering questions from other reporters. Mostly innocuous, repetitive ones about preparing for future races. Henrik's were the only spicy questions.

Everything went fast after that. Kirby gave her urine sample. Then it was time to celebrate.

In their designated changing area, Apollo picked her up and swung her around. Lindsey and a few other athletes were jumping around and cheering, and it was a big pit of hugs and excitement.

Apollo was beaming and acting as excited as if he'd won a gold medal. He'd unexpectedly made the final, which was thrilling.

And that was the cool thing about their sport. You raced against your competitors, but it was also an individual challenge. Every skier had their own personal goals. Their own demons to overcome.

Once the celebration settled, Lindsey gave Kirby a side hug.

"No Mara?" Kirby asked, even though she knew she shouldn't. Mara didn't do the team shit and celebrations.

"She bailed in the middle of the semifinals."

"Bummer." Kirby put a fake smile on. Mara had a regimented schedule. Watching your secret booty call win a bronze medal clearly did not fit in between light cardio, lunch, weight training, and yoga.

"She just doesn't like sharing the podium attention."

"Oh, I don't think..." Kirby genuinely hoped Mara would be happy for her, but she knew she shouldn't come to Mara's aid. It would be too revealing. Too strange. "She was happy for you to win your silver. Disappointed about falling, but happy for you."

Lindsey shrugged. "Mara's a mystery. It's almost time for the medal ceremony. You need to get in your podium outfit."

It was the third time Kirby had made an Olympic podium. If someone had asked seventeen-year-old Kirby what her life would look like as an adult, she would have said she would be working somewhere in her hometown. The tag agency or the diner or maybe, if she was lucky, the school. She would still be stuck in her dysfunctional and bigoted family's orbit.

She would never have imagined she would be stepping up onto the Olympic podium with a bronze around her neck, waving a bouquet of flowers, and trying not to cry.

CHAPTER
TWENTY-ONE

MARA WAS HIDING.

From her dad, who had started messaging the night before the ten-kilometer freestyle. He had a new job opportunity and wanted it to look as if he had her stamp of approval.

From her mom, who just wanted to make sure she was eating and getting enough sleep.

She was hiding from Lindsey, who had apologized for being snippy. The Olympics were stressful and didn't bring out people's best. According to Lindsey.

Mara certainly hadn't been bringing out her best. She felt out of sorts. Trash talking and fucking up interviews. Sleeping with Kirby. Freaking out over every simple thought in her head that almost, maybe, barely winked at being a *feeling*.

She was even hiding from Coach Karlsson, shutting down in the practice run for the freestyle ten-k when it didn't go particularly well. Coach Karlsson kept trying to go over the turns and course breakdown, but Mara had been a brick wall.

And she was hiding from Kirby. From thoughts of Kirby. Hiding from the press clips going around where Kirby said things like, *"it's a lot sweeter defeating the best,"* and *"I would know,"* and *"Mara doesn't matter."*

Mara locked everything away. The good stuff, like the defiant interviews and kisses and the tenderness that had bloomed between them. The stuff that had made her feel free for the first time in ages. She locked away the closeness and friendship she'd been developing with Jordan, and Brandilyn, and Lindsey. It was too scary.

And she hid from the bad too.

She hid from her performance in the ten-k interval start. She'd been in a weird headspace, and everything had suffered. It had felt messy and imprecise. She'd tried new sunglasses. A green pair. But they'd felt loose as she'd skied, and she knew she wouldn't wear them again.

She'd won a bronze. Another bronze.

She had enough to decorate a Christmas tree with them.

Mara should have been happy with a bronze. And, outwardly, she was. It wasn't an unexpected result. Most betting pools would have forecast her to place fourth or fifth, so some would say she'd outperformed expectations.

But Mara wanted a gold. She wanted to win every race she started.

As she stepped up on the podium, the lowest platform, and listened to the Swedish national anthem play for the gold medalist, Mara's mind strayed to Kirby's medal ceremony two days before.

Mara had watched it on silent on her phone, with the covers pulled over her head, so Lindsey wouldn't see or hear.

Kirby had cried happy tears during her medal ceremony. And Mara had wished she'd seen her race the finals. Mara would never get that back, would never be able to change the fact she'd left.

She'd never get the two days between back, where she'd isolated herself.

Queen of compartmentalization. Of hiding. Of being alone.

But the isolation wasn't working this time around. The quiet didn't feel healing. It felt lonely and bad.

Mara stepped onto the ski treadmill. She didn't love conditioning on the ski tread, much preferring to train on snow, but the coaches and physios were wanting to check her body alignment and hips. Her hip flexor had hurt since she'd finished the ten kilometer.

As she started skiing on the treadmill, she pulled her schedule up in her mind like a security blanket.

One day until Kirby raced the relay.

Five days until Kirby raced the team sprint with Brandilyn.

Nine days until the fifty-k.

One day. Five days. Nine days.

Kirby's events. Her event.

She only had one Olympic race left.

"Focus, Mara," Coach Karlsson said, voice clipped and gruff as always. "Try not to hide from the chance of pain when you activate that leg. You're shying away because you think it might hurt."

It was true.

She was hiding from the chance of pain. She was shying away from the possibility of being hurt.

Physically.

Emotionally.

"There. That's better," the physio said as Mara adjusted. "Feel okay?"

Her hip twinged at first, but then she pushed past it. She nodded.

After a few minutes, Coach Karlsson shut the ski tread-mill down, and Mara caught her breath.

She looked up, and Kirby was across the room, leaning against the doorway, openly watching her.

Coach Karlsson followed Mara's gaze and turned around. "Hello, KB. What are you doing here?"

"Checking out my competition."

Kirby was layered up like she'd been outside. Her coat was black and luxe. She wasn't dressed to ski, and Mara wondered where she'd been. And who she'd been with. And what she'd been doing. *And, and, and.*

Mara wanted to know everything.

"When will you be done, Mara?" Kirby asked. It was a neutral question asked with no emotions or teasing or hints.

Mara was used to the open, dramatic Kirby. Not this unreadable version.

"Now."

Coach Karlsson looked between them. "What do you need, KB?"

Kirby shook her head and shrugged. "Nothing from

you. I was hoping to chat with Mara." Kirby pulled sunglasses off her head. *The* sunglasses. The black ones Mara had bought her. Kirby spun them around her fingers deliberately. "I have some questions."

Uncomfortable silence settled in the room.

Kirby had searched her out. Kirby had *found* her. It had always been the opposite.

Mara's heart started to race. Kirby was basically waving the sunglasses at Mara, and it couldn't have been clearer what Kirby was asking for. What she needed.

"I'll be right there, Bonham."

Kirby's eyes seemed to flash at hearing her last name. She turned on her heel and headed toward the locker room. Mara felt breathless, and it wasn't from the training.

She hurried through getting unhooked from the treadmill.

Coach Karlsson casually moved closer. "You good, Mara?"

"Of course. My hip is fine."

"I wasn't talking about your hip. You seem…" Coach Karlsson cocked his head like he was measuring his words carefully. "You did great in the ten-k. I'm proud of you."

His words were a blow. They hit Mara out of nowhere. She wasn't able to barricade herself from the way they made her feel. Coach Karlsson was *proud* of her.

It wasn't a phrase they used. Their coach-skier relationship was based on respect, goals, and improvement. Not gushy stuff like being proud. Coach Karlsson was the least sentimental person she knew. That was why they worked so well together.

"Thanks. I should have placed higher."

"No. You did good." He frowned. "You're allowed to be happy, you know."

Mara clenched her teeth to stop the rush of emotions. Happiness. Joy. Sadness.

Everyone wanted her to open her heart and *feel*. And she just couldn't. Because if she did, it would all snowball. The Olympics weren't the place for an emotional awakening.

Mara nodded at Coach Karlsson, said goodbye to the others in the room, and went to find Kirby.

Kirby was alone in the locker room, looking at her phone. She'd taken her coat off, and Mara could see she was in one of the many Olympic uniforms they'd received. It was the one they were supposed to wear during inter-views, so it was easy to assume that's where Kirby had been. She had on makeup too. Her cheeks were sparkly.

"Hi," Mara said, and Kirby jumped like she hadn't real-ized Mara had come in.

"Hi."

"Are you… Do you need something?" Mara asked. That was why Mara searched out Kirby. Because she *needed*.

Needed connection. Needed the heat and excitement and freedom of letting herself be fully herself. Needed release. Needed to fight.

But she had no idea what Kirby needed.

"No. I just—I don't know," Kirby said warily.

Mara sat beside her. It had been one hundred and forty hours since they'd spoken, and Mara had so much to say stored up inside her. But she couldn't allow any of it to come out.

"I was watching our condom unboxing video earlier. I got asked about it in an interview. Got asked about you, of course," Kirby said. She seemed reserved and aloof. It was strange.

"What did you say?"

"Something biting and off-color. You'll hate it, which means you'll also love it. But it wasn't what I wanted to say."

"What did you want to say?"

Kirby scooted closer, their hips touching. "That I can't stop thinking about this." She lifted her phone and pressed Play.

In the video, Kirby launched herself at a laughing Mara, pinning her to a couch in the lounge and kissing the hell out of her.

"Oh, God." Mara could hardly watch. She'd known that was on video, that Kirby had a clip of it on her phone. But there were so many other things vying for attention in her brain that she'd barely given it a second thought.

"I've watched it a bunch of times," Kirby said.

Mara frowned and looked at Kirby. "Are you okay?"

"Yeah. Maybe not. I don't know. I feel weird. Don't you feel weird?"

Mara didn't know how to respond to that. She carried low-level discomfort on her like a base layer, so of course she felt weird.

But she didn't want Kirby to. Maybe she would be able to take Kirby's mind off the weirdness, to set her at ease and get her back on track.

Mara checked the room to make sure they were alone.

She brushed Kirby's hair behind her ear, and Kirby's eyes fluttered shut.

Mara followed her fingers with her lips, kissing Kirby's neck, her jaw. "We can't do this here, Bonham."

"Don't call me that."

Kirby. KB. Her name, her nickname. They had tasted so good, had felt so good when Mara allowed herself to say them, but she couldn't right then. She couldn't be that vulnerable. If Kirby needed to fuck, Mara could do that. If Kirby needed something deeper, she couldn't.

"Where can we go?" Mara asked, her lips at Kirby's ear.

Kirby grabbed the back of Mara's head, gripped it, and kissed her. It was all clashing lips and teeth for a few seconds before Kirby's incredible finesse kicked in, and she slowed way down. It was bone-quaking, gold-medal kissing.

The best kissing. It was as wonderful as the orgasms they'd shared. It was as wonderful as anything Mara had ever experienced. As *everything* she'd experienced.

Kirby backed off and stared at her warily.

"What do you think your life would be like if you hadn't become a cross-country ski racer?" Kirby asked.

"What? What do you mean?" Mara was still reeling from the kiss. She could hardly breathe, much less talk.

"If your life had zigged rather than zagging. Your parents sign you up for piano lessons instead of ski and voilà."

"Why are you asking that?"

"God, Mara. It's called a conversation." Kirby stood up, ripping herself away from Mara's greedy hands. "Don't you ever think about anything besides the competition and winning? Like where you'll enjoy skiing when this whole circus is done chewing us up and spitting us out. Who you would have been without skiing. Who you *will* be without it. I'm trying to make small talk with you."

Mara had no idea who she was without skiing. Without racing. She would find out soon enough, but she didn't want to worry about it yet.

"That's not small, and you know it."

"Okay, I'm trying to get to know you a tiny bit better."

"That's not what..." *That's not what this is.* Mara almost said it, but the words stuck in her throat. "I'd probably have married my high school boyfriend, had some kids, lived up in the fancy houses on the hillside in Anchorage. He's a cosmetic dentist now."

"You'd have such pretty veneers."

"Yes."

"Do you even like men?"

"Not particularly, no."

Kirby laughed, and it made Mara feel way too happy to make her smile. It wasn't good for Mara to be so invested in Kirby's laugh, in her happiness, her joyful smile.

"I don't want to talk about stuff like this," Mara said.

"Why?"

"We need to focus. *I* need to focus."

"And talking to me in an empty locker room is really cramping your intentionality, momentum, and rhythm? Or whatever nonsense buzz words you drop in interviews."

"Yeah, Bonham. It kind of is."

"Don't call me that."

Mara didn't like where this was going. She wasn't sure if it was the pressure cooker of the Olympics, or maybe it was her own hang-ups, but everything felt heavy. Every word. Every action. It had been building for days. Since her crash in the skiathlon. Maybe since their kisses in Oberhof after Kirby's panic attack.

And it was all getting mixed up in Mara's brain. Her plans and goals.

To craft her legacy.

To win gold.

To enjoy her last experience at the Olympics.

To do her best.

What was her real purpose here?

Surely, it wasn't… it *couldn't* be to fall for her biggest fucking rival. It just couldn't be.

Mara met Kirby's eyes. They were the brightest blue. Like a glacier-fed lake. And so wounded. So hurt, even though Mara hadn't pulled the trigger on their *situation* yet. But Kirby knew it was coming. She had to.

Mara refused to put her skiing at risk. This—*Kirby*—was taking up too much emotional bandwidth. Too much mental load.

"If you want to fuck again, let me know, but I'm not your emotional crutch, *Kirby*."

CHAPTER
TWENTY-TWO

HEAVY, oppressive silence filled the locker room.

Kirby should have known it was a mistake to talk to Mara.

I'm not your emotional crutch.

Kirby.

Yikes.

Kirby hadn't sought out Mara intentionally. She had just started to wander through the training areas, looking around, searching for something to calm the rabbiting of her heart. Someone to talk to. Somewhere she belonged.

It was a mistake to think Mara cared about more than a few quickies. Kirby didn't belong with Mara. Not in the same ski clubs. Not in a relationship.

"You know, we compete in such a physically agonizing sport. Pushing our bodies to collapse," Kirby said. "Pushing until we are in unimaginable pain. But you saying *that* might have hurt worse than anything I've ever felt while skiing." Kirby tried to speak as evenly as she could. She deserved to say her peace, whether Mara was mature enough to hear it or not.

"That seems… a little dramatic."

"Oh, fuck you."

Mara's spine went straight as a ski pole. She was in her training gear and as beautiful as ever. "No really. Why would that hurt? Why does it matter what I say now?"

Kirby paced away. She wanted to rip her own hair out. It felt like what they had, what they *could* have, was so obvious. But not to Mara May, who evidently only had skis for brains.

They hadn't spoken in days, and the separation felt like the full-body agony at the end of a race. She'd wanted to celebrate with Mara after winning her bronze medal. She'd wanted to commiserate with Mara after Mara had won hers because Kirby knew Mara wouldn't be happy with a bronze.

But Mara had avoided her like she had *before*.

Before they'd kissed. Before they'd fucked. Before the slow creep of vulnerability between them.

"If you can't answer that for yourself, then you are the most obtuse person I've ever met."

"It's not like we're, I don't know… You do this all the time," Mara said. "I thought it didn't mean anything to you. You said it was nothing."

"You're the literal worst."

"What did you expect? Don't you hook up with people all the time? How was I supposed to know I was any different than anyone else?"

"Real nice. Using my sexual history as a dig."

"It's not a dig!" Mara raised her voice. "I am genuinely asking. What have you ever said or done that would make me think it was anything besides blowing off steam? What did you say that day after the Janette Collins interview? You wanted hot and meaningless. That's what I thought this was. Yes, we're compatible in bed, but that doesn't mean you have feelings for me."

"If you can't tell, then you're—"

"That's unfair," Mara interrupted. "The most important thing to me was competing. This"—she gestured between them—"is not something I am willing to lose sleep over right now."

"Yes, God forbid I have a feeling. Sorry that's so inconvenient for you."

"I thought we were on the same page. You've been saying the same shit about me in interviews," Mara snapped.

"And you've been giving it right back. I thought we… I thought it was understood. That it was—"

"A game?"

It was a game. But Kirby's feelings didn't feel like a game anymore.

"Yeah."

"Yes," Mara snarled. "And I love joking about the worst day of my life. How fun for me."

"Losing one race. What a privilege for that to be your worst day. Give me a break." Kirby felt done and *mean*. It wasn't a good combo. It hadn't served her well in relationships in the past.

Mara's cheeks were red, and her body seemed geared up to fight. She was tight as a bowstring and practically shaking. Not the cold, little princess after all.

Kirby crowded her against one of the fancy wooden lockers. They were both breathing hard. Mara licked her lips, and Kirby wanted to kiss her. She wanted to pin Mara to the wall, bite the join of her neck and shoulder, and make her come apart.

"You know what?" Kirby whispered, venom in her voice. She touched a curl of Mara's hair that had fallen over her shoulder. One last touch. "You're right. You're not worth losing focus over. Or spending time on. And just to be clear, you've been using me as your emotional crutch for twelve days, since that very first time, princess. So I wanted to exchange a few pleasantries before reducing you to nothing but a begging hot mess. Sue me. And grow up."

A throat cleared. "Umm."

Kirby jerked away from Mara at the sound, and Mara basically threw herself across the room. It would have been funny if Kirby had been capable of accessing her sense of humor at that moment.

Lindsey was standing in the doorway, her sports bag in her hand. Her eyes were as wide as saucers.

"Hi," Kirby said. Cold sweat broke out on Kirby's back, and adrenaline made her ears ring.

"Hi." Lindsey glanced between them. "So."

"No." Mara shook her head, one quick jerk. "No."

Kirby felt upset. But Mara *looked* upset. She wasn't hiding it. It was a douse of cold water to see Mara's live reaction to being romantically associated with Kirby. Not exactly a confidence boost.

"*No* what?" Lindsey said very slowly. "I didn't, you know, *see or hear anything very wild and out of the ordinary.*"

"No," Mara repeated. "I can't… No."

Kirby wanted to come to Mara's rescue. But she didn't. Mara was a big girl.

"I guess, umm." Lindsey turned to Kirby. "I could give you guys a few more minutes."

"It's fine. I'm done here," Kirby said coldly.

"*Kirby,*" Mara said, her voice soft.

"Uh-uh. Don't call me that now," Kirby said.

"Yeah, I'm gonna go," Lindsey said.

"Nah." Kirby shrugged. "I am."

———

"Mara, sit down," Lindsey said gently.

Mara was poised like she was about to burst off the starting line. She felt cornered, but she didn't know if she wanted to race after Kirby or run and hide.

"I just…" Mara twitched but couldn't make her feet move. "I think I…" *Messed up. Ruined something.*

"You're okay. Sit down." Lindsey pushed her onto a bench. The same bench she'd been kissing Kirby on.

Mara popped back up like the seat had burned her.

"So if you're having an emotional breakdown, let me know," Lindsey said. "We have support for mental health stuff."

"I'm not. I'm fine." *Debatable.* "Nine more days."

"What?" Lindsey said. "Do I need to go get a coach?"

"There's nine days to the fifty-k."

"Yeah."

"One day to the relay. Five to the team sprint." Mara paced across the room. She tried to control her breathing.

"You're not in those races."

"I know. Kirby is. That's Kirby's schedule. And my schedule. It's the... schedule."

"Yeah, I'm going to get a coach."

"No!" Mara sat down beside her. "I'm fine."

Super debatable. She'd never had a breakup like that before. Was it a breakup if it hadn't been real to begin with?

But it had been real to *Kirby*.

How and when had that happened? How had Mara missed it?

If she checked her biometrics on her fancy smartwatch, it would probably look like she'd had a heart attack or something. Her whole body felt like an exposed nerve.

"How are things with you and Apollo?" Mara asked. She didn't know what else to say.

"Holy fuck, Mara. I am not talking about boys with you right now."

"Okay."

Lindsey stared at her. Mara stared at her feet.

"Hey," Lindsey said. Then Lindsey hugged her, and nothing could have shocked Mara more.

Tears sprung to her eyes, but she blinked them away. "Oh, no." She squeezed Lindsey back and held on.

"It's going to be okay. I don't know what all that was, but it's going to be okay."

Mara nodded against Lindsey's shoulder.

"You deserve to be celebrated and loved on for your last season, Mara. It's a big deal. Your retirement. Your last Olympics. Have you seen the Instagram posts? So many people are posting tributes and memories for you. I love KB. She's fun and a great teammate, but don't let her drag you into drama either. Don't let her ruin this for you. Focus on your Olympics, and lock in."

"She didn't drag me."

"All right."

"I wanted these Olympics to be fun." That comment fell between them like a lead balloon.

Lindsey laughed. And that made Mara laugh too.

Mara pulled back. "I sound so unhinged right now. I feel so unhinged."

"You're not known for being fun."

"No."

Lindsey smiled. "It's a good thing to want, though. I'll tell you what—let's watch figure skating tonight. It's the men's free skate. That will be fun."

"You're sure?" Mara wanted that. "Don't you have training?" She was calming down. All the defense mechanisms clicking back into place.

She had fucked up with Kirby. Mara had started it, but Kirby had proven why she was so good on reality TV by finishing it.

"No, it was optional. Let's go," Lindsey said before

ushering Mara back to their room. Mara was in a daze and let herself be led.

Somehow, Lindsey magicked up grilled chicken, pasta, salad, and cannoli, and Mara ate it without thinking about the nutritional content.

"This might be the best thing I've ever put in my mouth," Mara said, after demolishing the cannoli.

"That sounded so dirty, but I don't feel like I can make a joke about it," Lindsey said.

"Why not?"

"Because you're about to cry."

Mara sighed. She wasn't about to cry, but it felt like she was viewing the world through static.

"Do you want to talk about it?" Lindsey asked. "I'm all ears. I won't tell anyone."

"Not even Apollo?"

Lindsey glanced down at her phone. "He's with KB. He texted earlier. Said she needed him."

"Is she okay?"

Lindsey smiled. "He keeps Kirby's secrets."

Mara set her plate aside and fell back on the bed. "Ugh. What a melodrama we have going on here."

"At the worst time too. Poor judgment by all of us."

Mara laughed, but it came out more like a dry cough. "Yeah, what were we thinking?"

"Well, I was thinking that I couldn't keep leading Apollo on without being honest about my feelings because he'd eventually fall in love with Kirby, and then I'd be super sad."

"Oh." Mara knew Kirby and Apollo had hooked up before. Kirby had told her as much, but it had never occurred to Mara to be jealous about it. Mara and Kirby's chemistry had been so explosive. Addictive almost. It had been the ultimate distraction. And Kirby had seemed just as affected by it. So no, Mara hadn't been worried about Apollo.

"What were you thinking?" Lindsey asked.

Mara covered her face. "I can't talk about it."

"No gossip. Got it."

Mara hadn't meant to hurt Kirby. She'd just wanted to stop feeling so turned around. So vulnerable. And she hadn't known how to tell her that without breaking everything to pieces.

"I shouldn't have left before seeing Kirby's sprint final."

"Everyone—the press, the coaches—they all act like you're some great leader because you're a great skier, but a leader wouldn't have left."

"I know." Mara swallowed the lump in her throat. "It freaked me out. I was so worked up, wanting her to do well. So worried. I was too invested. I'd felt like my body couldn't handle the stress."

"You probably read the endings of books first too."

"What?" Mara said. She'd known Lindsey a long time. She hoped they would be friends once this was over. But this was the deepest conversation they'd ever had, and Mara didn't quite know how to follow Lindsey's conversational detours.

"I think that hurt her. That you weren't there," Lindsey said. "She asked for you afterward."

"Aww, damn it." Mara pressed her palms to her eye sockets.

"It's okay to want to wait until after competition to figure your feelings out," Lindsey said. "Especially at the Olympics. Like, that makes sense, Mara. You deserve the time and space to focus and compete."

"Sure." Logically, that was the truth. Mara had been saying it from the beginning. To herself. To Kirby.

But emotions weren't logical. And Mara couldn't get around the fact that she had broken something worth keeping precious and safe.

Lindsey stood up. "Come on. Let's go watch figure skating. Maybe the lounge won't be too wild."

The lounge was a madhouse. American cross-country skiers and ski jumpers were all squished in around a large TV to watch the event. Luckily, Apollo and Kirby were nowhere to be seen. She was pretty sure she wouldn't be able to see Kirby without crying, fleeing, or starting another fight.

There had been watch parties in the lounge since the beginning of the Games, but the only time she'd been in there had been to film the condom unboxing video with Kirby. She sat on the same couch, in the same spot where Kirby had kissed her, and tried to focus on the screen. It was hard. She kept thinking back to that kiss. To every kiss.

Kirby had the video. It had been unnerving seeing how easily Kirby took her down in that clip. She'd been under Kirby's spell after nothing but a touch. She hadn't liked seeing the proof of it.

After Mara had distantly watched a few figure skaters

complete their programs, Brandilyn plopped into the spot beside her. Lindsey was still on Mara's other side, steady like a sentry.

"Hey, Mara May."

"Hi, Brandilyn. How's the knee?"

"Shaky."

"I'm so sorry," Mara said. "Will you race in the relay?"

"Yeah. I don't want to let the team down. And who knows? I might not ever get a chance at the Olympics again. I don't want to miss it."

Mara turned to her. "You'll get another chance. You're talented."

Brandilyn shrugged. "Not everyone does. Not everyone is like you. Or KB."

"I'm not... *You* can be. There's longevity in our sport if you take care of yourself. That's not something I've always been good at, but I hope you will be."

"The doctors said I can ski on the knee. It's just a little—"

"I don't mean your knee. I mean take care of yourself *here*." Mara tapped her own temple. "And here." She touched her own chest.

Brandilyn took that sappiness with as much seriousness as it deserved. Mara never doled out life or skiing advice, and Brandilyn clearly didn't know what to say. She nodded and immediately started chatting up a ski jumper who was sitting on the floor in front of the sofa.

Lindsey bumped her shoulder against Mara's. "Hey, hey, leader."

Mara brushed that off with a small smile. She'd taken

pains throughout her career to protect her peace, to isolate, to avoid every hard thought and feeling that didn't apply to racing better, to being better. Nothing mattered but being the best cross-country skier. But maybe being the best racer was about more than optimizing her body, her intervals, and her nutrition.

She needed to listen to her own advice and take care of her heart.

TWENTY-THREE

KIRBY FELT like she was moving through thick fog. Her legs were heavy, her head full of cotton.

Coach Wu was talking to her, and she was nodding along, but nothing was clicking. Other coaches moved around her relay partners, who were all pulling on their lucky relay socks, getting geared up. A wax tech was speaking to Jordan.

The mood in the changing room was electric. Relay days usually were, but she didn't feel anything but sad. Which was ridiculous. Being sad about Mara May was ridiculous.

Kirby had slept in Apollo's room, his roommate conveniently absent all night, but Apollo snored. And when he wasn't snoring, he'd been texting Lindsey with the click-clack sound of his phone's keyboard turned on. Kirby had wanted to wring his neck, but she also couldn't imagine being anywhere else.

"You've never acted like this about a relationship before," he'd said once she'd come clean. She'd denied that.

She'd pulled up examples from her dating shows. The breakup with her most recent ex had been full of drama—rumors, paparazzi photos, shade online, an explosive reunion episode, which would air the week after the Olympics—but Apollo knew her. He hadn't bought it.

Kirby's emotions were already jumbled and outsized from the excitement and pressure surrounding the Olympics, from the panic attacks that seemed to jump her at random moments, from the whiplash of going between filming and racing. Adding in the messiness of falling for Mara May had been like taking a match to gasoline. And her brain had decided it was too much. She was shutting down.

She couldn't snap out of it.

Coach Wu gripped her knee, and she jumped. "What?"

"What's up with you today?" Coach asked.

"Nothing."

Coach Wu shook her head. "You need to look alive, KB. Your teammates are depending on you."

"Okay. I know." Kirby slid her headband into place. Coach Wu left without another word. She'd seemed disappointed.

Kirby closed her eyes and took a deep breath. She needed to focus. She needed to lock in. She couldn't be a disappointment.

Someone squatted down in front of her, and Kirby expected it to be a coach. She opened her eyes, ready to fake it. To fake being pumped up. To fake being fine.

It was Mara May.

Mara rarely assisted on her teammates' race days. She

rarely showed up. But there she was, lugging a carrier of water bottles. She handed Kirby's to her.

"You race better mad," Mara said, her voice soft but full of steel. "You race better with a chip on your shoulder."

"I swear to God if that's why you—"

"Of course it's not. But you need to go out there and show me exactly how fucking mad you are. Make me regret not racing in this relay with you, Bonham."

Fire zipped through Kirby because it did make her mad. She was furious at Mara—and kind of heartbroken—but mostly just outrageously livid.

"There you are," Mara whispered. She picked up the sunglasses that were beside Kirby on the bench. They were the black ones Mara had gotten her. She'd worn them for every race, every run, every practice since Mara had left them in her room.

Mara gingerly put the sunglasses on the top of Kirby's head like she was scared to touch her.

Then Mara left without another word, moving on to give Brandilyn, who was rubbing balm onto her knee, a water bottle and a mini peptalk.

Kirby tracked Mara around the room as she spoke with everyone. She was unsmiling, cold, and businesslike. She didn't linger with anyone but chatted with all four relay skiers.

"Let's fucking go," Kirby said to no one in particular. But everyone shouted like she'd given a speech. Jordan banged her hands on the bench in a drumroll. Coach Wu nodded to Kirby from across the room. And Mara walked to the doorway, turned, met Kirby's eyes for a brief second, and left.

The sun sparkled off the sheets of perfect snow as they made their way outside. Kirby knocked the sunglasses from her forehead down over her eyes. The sky was clear blue. The energy in the stadium was charged.

Relay days were special.

Kirby was usually humming with excitement and adrenaline before a relay. But instead, she was fuming. They skied their warm-ups, and then, before Kirby knew it, Jordan was off on the lead-off scramble leg. The crowd's cheers were earsplitting.

Kirby often raced the third leg, with Brandilyn pulling the anchor, since they were both strongest at the freestyle versus the classic style of the first two legs. But with Brandilyn's injury, the coaches had switched them around. Kirby had to bide her time and stay warm and primed through three legs.

She had to stay *angry* through three legs. The sound of the crowd faded in her head as the first and second legs transitioned in the relay exchange zone.

"You got this," Kirby said to Brandilyn. They hadn't practiced their exchange—Brandilyn tapping Kirby versus the other way around—as often as Kirby would have preferred, but it was going to be okay.

Kirby wasn't going to fuck this up for anyone else.

When Brandilyn was tapped to start her leg, the US was in sixth. Brandilyn was a great pursuit racer, though. She raced better when chasing someone.

Kirby moved into position in the relay exchange zone.

She slowed her breathing and tugged on that thread of anger. It was sharp and red, a consistent drumbeat in her chest.

Fuck Mara. Fuck everyone.

Brandilyn came back into view. They were still in sixth, but she had closed the gap significantly, and all the top teams were clustered up.

Kirby started skiing when Brandilyn was a few meters away. Then she felt the tap on her shoulder, and she burst forward, through the stadium and out onto the course, leaving the cheering crowds behind.

She focused on her skis and poles, on skiing hard and clean, and on the skier in front of her.

Fuck everyone.

Kirby pushed up a hill, drawing level with her first victim. She passed the German skier. Hills were her favorite. So hard, so much effort.

The next skier came into her sights.

Her legs burned. Her chest burned.

She gained ground on the downhill and hit the final curve and straightaway back into the stadium.

She pulled into fourth. Third place—Finland—was within reach.

She was going to finish this hard. No one would ever say again that she wasn't focused. That her attention, and ambition, and drive were split between skiing and the reality TV, influencer shit.

Fuck Mara. Fuck everyone.

She could do both. She *would* do both.

She wasn't the princess of cross-country skiing, but she was the workhorse.

CHAPTER
TWENTY-FOUR

THE SOUND STAGE WAS BRIGHT. Mara always forgot how bright TV studios were.

She had her bronze medal around her neck. Lindsey had the silver around hers.

And Kirby had two bronzes around hers.

Mara felt breathless just thinking about Kirby on that straightaway coming into the stadium during the relay. She'd never looked faster.

When Kirby had crossed the finish line, she'd screamed. A primal, visceral scream that Mara had felt in her bones. Mara wanted a frame of that scream on her wall. She wanted to live in its echo.

Janette Collins shook all their hands before sitting down on the couch opposite them. Her co-anchor, Michael Johnstone, smiled at them. He was a kind and gentle foil to Janette Collins's sharkiness.

Mara had been interviewed by both over the years. Janette more recently. Michael during the Beijing Olympics.

"This evening, we have the three veteran medalists on the Women's US Cross-Country Ski Team," Janette said. "We spoke yesterday with the whole relay team about their emotional third place finish, but we wanted to highlight the historic nature of these Games by talking to the racers who have the experience to understand its impact."

Mara smiled like she was supposed to at that. She glanced at Kirby. Lindsey was between them on the couch.

They hadn't spoken since before the relay. Kirby had mouthed "Thank you" during the celebration after the bronze, but Mara hadn't gotten close since then.

She'd wanted to. But she also couldn't imagine putting herself, or Kirby, through that again.

"Were you expecting the US Cross-Country Ski Team to come home with so many medals?" Janette asked. "With the potential for more on the horizon, by the way, with the team sprint and the fifty-kilometer mass start still upcoming."

Mara didn't answer, hoping someone else would. Kirby could typically be relied on for that.

"We all want to do our best," Lindsey said. "And often our best is medal worthy. But things have to align. There are a lot of variables in cross-country skiing."

It was a perfect, media-trained answer.

"Mara, as the veteran here with the most Olympic starts, and the most lifetime Olympic medals, why do you think these Games have been so special?" Michael asked.

"Kirby will pass me," Mara said. "On the medal front."

That didn't answer the question, and she wasn't sure why she'd said it.

Both women on the couch looked at her, but Kirby turned away quickly.

"I mean." Mara's face got hot. She didn't know what it was about speaking to the press lately. She just couldn't say the right thing. "I think she will. Eventually."

"We have a lot of tenacity," Lindsey said, taking the focus from Mara. Thank God for friends. "A lot of fight on this team. Mara and Kirby are a great example. They have this rivalry that's momentous. They push each other to be better."

Michael asked a few meatball questions about training and teamwork. Lindsey answered the majority of them. Mara added a rote answer here or there. Kirby didn't say a word.

"KB," Janette said, her eyes a bit narrow. It was supposed to be a fluffy interview, but Mara was worried Janette had smelled blood in the water and wouldn't hesitate to bite. "You haven't said much. Are you looking forward to the team sprint? The unfortunate news dropped today that Brandilyn Rogers won't be skiing it with you."

"Yes. I'm looking forward to it."

Mara frowned, confused by Kirby's demeanor. She'd watched every interview Kirby had done since getting bronze in the relay. Kirby had been her usual sly and playful self. It might have been a front, but Mara didn't think so.

Kirby had moved on, moved past their personal upheaval.

So Mara didn't understand why Kirby was acting so strange now.

"Do you know yet who will race the team sprint with you?" Michael asked.

Kirby shook her head. "Not yet. The coaches are figuring it out."

"Well, there are two incredibly fast racers next to you. Could it be either of you ladies?" he asked of Lindsey and Mara.

It was a well-meaning question, but Lindsey wasn't a sprinter, and Mara had been focusing on distance races for years. She raced sprints on the World Cup circuit, and raced them well, but it wasn't her priority.

Lindsey laughed. "KB does not want it to be me. We have many, many skiers who are better suited to that event."

Mara didn't know what to say. It would be the coaches' decision, and they would never ask her.

"The US Ski Team likes to focus on the individual needs of racers," Kirby said. Her voice was wobbly. "We're all different. We have different training needs, off-season needs, and competition needs. Once in race mode, I get better through the course of competition, with repetitive starts. If I take breaks that are too long, too many days apart, I lose momentum and that killer instinct, so I prefer to compete in as many events as I can. I don't want to speak for Mara, but I think it's fair to say that she's different. She needs different things. She skis better with rest, recovery, and mental and emotional space between events. Her focus is and should be the fifty-k. I would never want to jeopardize that."

It was a decent answer but devoid of the humor and

cleverness Kirby was known for. It honestly didn't sound like her at all.

I would never want to jeopardize that.

It was a loaded response, full of double meaning only Mara and Kirby understood.

And Mara's first thought, one she didn't say out loud, wasn't like her at all either.

Let's race. I would race with you.

Mara leaned forward so she could better see Kirby on the other side of Lindsey.

Kirby's hands were clenched in her lap, and her jaw was tight. She swallowed a few times like she had something stuck in her throat.

Mara stood up, and everyone in the studio reacted in surprise. She sat back down.

"Sorry. Can we take a second, please? A break. This isn't live. Can I have a second? Off the record or whatever," Mara asked.

The producer off-camera said, "I guess."

And Mara jumped back up. She went to Kirby, kneeled in front of her, and grabbed her hands. They weren't cramped up like Mara had expected them to be.

"Are you okay?" Mara asked. She rubbed Kirby's hands roughly anyway.

"I'm fine." Kirby glanced around, checking everyone's reactions. Mara didn't care about anyone else's reaction.

"Are you sure? I'll cause a scene, and we can end the interview if you need me to."

"You're causing a scene already, babe," Kirby said, drollness creeping into her voice.

"You seemed… I thought—"

Kirby almost smiled. "I know what you thought, Mara. I wasn't having a panic attack."

Lindsey stood up and moved away, giving them the illusion of space.

"I'm so sorry, Kirby." Mara squeezed Kirby's hands.

"About stopping the interview?"

"No. About everything else."

Kirby pulled her hands slowly out of Mara's. "Now's not the best time for apologies." She looked pointedly at everyone watching them openly.

"I think I'm bad at interviews," Mara said.

"No shit. But you're also sometimes really good at them."

"You might rather have Jordan, but I would race with you. In the team sprint."

Kirby immediately started shaking her head. "You're being very fucking weird right now, Mara."

"So?"

That seemed to throw Kirby. She stared at Mara, her brows furrowed. Mara wasn't the best at reading people, but Kirby seemed extra inscrutable.

Kirby finally looked over Mara's head toward the producer and said, "We can keep going."

Mara couldn't do anything but sit back down in her seat. But she didn't want to sit in *her* seat. She sat in Lindsey's so she was closer to Kirby.

"So can we ask what that was about?" Janette asked before the cameras were rolling.

Kirby took a shaky breath. "Sure."

They all got settled again, and Janette immediately jumped into it. "We just took a small break from filming. It seemed as if Mara and KB had something important to discuss and asked to do so off camera. Can you explain what's going on, Mara?"

Mara ground her teeth together. "No." It wasn't her story to tell.

"She thought I was about to have a panic attack. She was checking on me," Kirby said. "Everyone thinks we hate each other, but Mara actually is a kind person. She's seen me have one before and thought I was showing similar signs. She was being a good teammate."

"A panic attack?" Michael said, concern etched on his face. "Have you ever spoken about having panic attacks before?"

"No," Kirby said uneasily. "I probably should have used my position and celebrity to advocate for mental health causes and stuff but—"

"That's not your responsibility. It's okay to just live your journey, Kirby," Mara said. "It's no one's business unless you want it to be."

"Says the ice princess," Kirby said wryly.

"Hey."

"I don't like to talk about it because I don't feel like I've got a handle on them. Sometimes I'll go months or even years without one. Sometimes I'll have a few a week. I had two during pre-Olympic training and one this morning during breakfast in the cafeteria."

Ah. She hadn't been about to have an attack. She was coming down from one.

"Does something trigger them?" Janette asked.

Kirby shrugged. "No. I don't know. Stress. Bad sleep. Overactive thyroid. Too much coffee. A combo of multiple factors. I've never been able to pinpoint it. Our sports psych said it could be lots of things, and I've got doctors' appointments scheduled for after the Olympics. But my mental health is part of my overall health story. It's a difficulty we all contend with, and the team does a great job providing resources. I appreciate Mara being concerned for me and for the chance to explain, but I'm fine."

"Thank you for being so open about it, KB," Michael said.

"Without going too inside baseball, or rather inside cross-country skiing here, I interviewed Mara and KB together during training before they came to Italy," Janette said. "It was one of the most interesting and perhaps contentious interviews I've ever done. It hasn't aired yet, but it will air before the fifty-kilometer race in a few days. It is a bit shocking to see the difference between how Mara checked on you during this interview and how you two fought during that one."

"We're teammates," Lindsey said, clearly jumping in and all over the question. Because she *was* a very, very good teammate. "We're competitors, and that can get tense, but we also care about each other."

Kirby's knee bumped Mara's on the couch. It might have been unintentional, but it reverberated through her whole body.

"Mara and I are not best friends," Kirby said. "I'd say there have been lots of times where we were quite *unfriendly* even. Rivals. Enemies. Those instances are well-documented, including in your interview. But she's motivating. She pisses me off more than just about anyone in the world, but pursuing her, catching her… *in a race…* is very motivating."

An ache of something—aggravation or longing or discomfort—pulsed through Mara's chest. Her breath sped up, and she had to force herself not to touch Kirby, not to grab her.

"Mara, what do you have to say to that?" Janette asked.

I like being pursued. I like being caught.

"Nothing."

A laugh snapped out of Kirby, and Mara couldn't keep her smile in. A real smile, not the media-trained one. Not her podium smile.

"I get the feeling you guys enjoy messing around with each other," Michael said.

And then Lindsey laughed. And Mara wanted to bury her head in her hands because he really had no idea how apt that statement was.

KIRBY SHOWED up early at the training facility to practice for the team sprint. When she came into the weight room, she shouldn't have been surprised to see Mara geared up and stretching, but she was.

Their interview with Lindsey had been such a mess. A funny mess. A frustrating one.

Kirby felt burned by Mara's whiplash. She had read comments online about the interview. Clips had been posted all over social media. She'd reposted them. There was speculation about dissent among the ski team and speculation about them playing up their animosity for clicks. Rumors fed headlines and headlines fed her. So she was perfectly happy with a bit of gossip.

But if she thought about the care Mara had shown her, about how Mara had acted so out of the ordinary *for Kirby*, she would start to think and wish and hope for things that were definitely off the table.

"Weaseled your way into the team sprint after all?"

Kirby said. Mara had offered during that interview, but Kirby hadn't taken her seriously. What she'd said about skiers needing different things was true. Mara *did* ski better if she had time to prepare. If she stuck with a schedule and routine of race, recovery, rest, repeat.

"Yeah," Mara said with a shrug. She changed stretching positions, so self-possessed and fluidly elegant.

"You didn't have to do that. If you felt some obligation because…" They weren't alone. The coaches were milling around. She couldn't say why Mara might have felt obligated, but the flash in Mara's eyes showed she'd caught Kirby's meaning.

"I don't feel obligated. I was the best option. I just made sure the coaches understood that." She spoke with such unbelievable arrogance.

"I don't want you to risk your legs for the fifty."

"You don't need to worry about my legs, Bonham," Mara said pointedly. "Worry about yourself."

"That's enough, Mara," the head coach, Coach Redman, said, not looking up from his notebook. Coach Wu winked at Kirby from behind his back. "We have to practice the exchange. Kirby you'll anchor."

And that was what they did. Kirby didn't have much choice.

No, that wasn't true.

She could have argued it. She could have claimed that she deserved to race with someone she had chemistry with, who she felt comfortable with. The team sprint was a team effort between just two skiers. They needed to be in sync, to trust each other.

But after practicing their exchange a few times, no one would have believed they didn't have racing chemistry.

They'd never raced the team sprint together. By the time Kirby had come up and earned her spot in the team sprint, Mara had dropped the event.

Mara loved the sufferfest of endurance and distance. She excelled there. But as she zipped around the track at about seventy-five percent effort, Kirby couldn't deny that she still had it. She still had that sprint instinct and muscle memory locked in.

And their exchanges were seamless. Smooth. No friction or issues at all. It was honestly frustrating. They could have been dominating in the event for years.

After practice they found themselves alone in the locker room once again. Mara didn't look up as she changed.

Kirby finished dressing first and watched Mara meticulously fold and put every piece of training gear and clothing away in her bag. She was so particular.

She had her sunglasses up on her head. A new pair that were pastel blue. They fell off her head and bounced across the room when she bent down to take off her socks.

Mara flinched and froze.

Kirby picked them up and examined them, déjà vu hitting her hard. She remembered silver sunglasses falling to the floor in her Oberhof apartment. She remembered carefully placing those glasses on top of Mara's head. "They're fine."

"Okay."

Kirby tried to hand the blue sunglasses back, but Mara just stared at them in Kirby's palm.

Kirby didn't know how to fix their relationship. Or if she should even try.

She set the glasses on the bench, and Mara grabbed them.

"Thank you," Kirby said.

"For what?"

"For racing with me."

"Don't thank me yet. I could choke."

Kirby considered her for a long moment. "You might."

"*Thanks.*"

"Or I could break a pole. Or one of us could fall. Or get a terrible case of shingles tonight. Or break an ankle getting off the shuttle. Or a sink hole could swallow us up right before the finish line."

Mara glanced up, her eyes wide. She was so superstitious, and it was too fun to needle her.

"If you choke, you choke," Kirby said. "It would be okay." They won as a team, they choked as a team. And sometimes, truly, the most important thing wasn't winning.

"No, it wouldn't."

Kirby huffed a laugh at Mara's cheerlessness. "It was fun. Practice today was fun." They had both been grim-faced and way too serious, but every time Kirby tapped Mara's shoulder, it felt *right*.

Mara nodded, as solemn and earnest as always. "Yes."

———

Kirby was locked in. She'd slept well. Eaten well. There was that calm in her body that was rare, the calm she craved.

She was usually jittery. Full of energy or anger. Full of some emotion that made her edgy and wound up and itching to *go*.

Mara hadn't smiled once, her race face on. A mask. Armor.

She had on her silver sunglasses. The ones from *that day*. The ones Jordan had borrowed, and Mara had retrieved. The ones Kirby had placed back on Mara's head after they'd had sex.

Kirby didn't mention it.

In fact, she didn't say anything. They hadn't said a word to each other.

Kirby knew what most of her teammates needed before a relay or team sprint, but she didn't know what Mara needed besides quiet. They pulled on their lucky relay socks, a symbol of unity.

As they got ready to enter the stadium, Mara looked over at her and frowned. "Do I need to insult you or something?"

"What?" Kirby asked, unable to hold in her smile.

"Should I make you mad? You race better mad, right?"

"Just being near you makes me mad. You're good."

Mara's lips nearly curled at the edges. "Cool."

Kirby couldn't even hear the crowd as she and Mara came into the stadium. She could only hear the smile in Mara's voice reverberating in her ears.

The team sprint opened with a qualification round with an interval start, each lead-off skier leaving in thirty-second increments. They would each do one lap in the qualification round, and the fastest fifteen teams would move on to a final heat consisting of six laps, three for each skier on a team.

For the qualification round, Mara took off at her signal with such power. It was beautiful to watch. Much like the sprint, they needed to qualify but also leave gas in the tank for the final heat.

Kirby moved into the relay exchange zone. In less than three minutes, Mara came back into view on the straight-away. She was flying. She tapped Kirby, a smooth exchange, just like practice.

And Kirby flew too.

CHAPTER
TWENTY-SIX

MARA HAD TWO MINUTES.

Two minutes of standing beside Kirby before being forced to move to the starting line. Two minutes to say something before the final heat. To say anything.

Kirby had her eyes closed and was moving from one leg to the other. She kept shaking out her arms. They had hardly spoken after they'd come in with the fifth best time in the qualification leg. Kirby had nodded at her. Mara had nodded back.

It had been silence since then.

One minute.

She could hear people in the stands chanting her name. There were a lot of American flags waving.

She watched Kirby, but Kirby didn't open her eyes.

Thirty seconds. She didn't know what she should say. She wanted to say something.

They were given the signal to head to the start, and Kirby finally looked at her.

Kirby reached out and moved Mara's sunglasses, which had been up on her head, down into position over her eyes.

"Thanks," Mara said.

Kirby nodded again.

And that was it. She should have said more. But that was it.

Mara wasn't an aggressive skier, and she'd never been the scramble leg on a relay or team sprint where she had to jockey for the best position once the race started.

But she understood the strategy. She wasn't going to let Kirby down.

The signal sounded, and she immediately bounded forward, making a tactical move to the front, and she was off.

Under three minutes. She needed to finish her lap in well under three minutes. Two and half would be better.

Easy.

There was only one skier in front of her.

She powered up the hill and flew down it, around a slick curve, and back onto the straightaway. The lap was just under a mile long. When she skated back into the stadium, Kirby was in the relay exchange zone.

Mara pushed, tapping Kirby on the shoulder as Kirby took off.

One leg down. Five to go.

Mara breathed through the exertion and prepared for her next leg, only a few minutes to recover. The team sprint was an interesting and complex mix of anaerobic and aerobic work, and her fitness skills were better suited to continuous endurance and distance, but that didn't matter today. She was going to succeed even if it shredded every muscle in her body.

Kirby raced into the stadium. She was in third but barely. All three top teams were bunched up.

She tapped Mara.

Mara burst forward and quickly swung around the sprinter from Italy, putting first place—Norway—in her sights.

She finished her lap in second, and Kirby zipped off.

One lap left. Mara only had one lap left. Then it was all on Kirby to finish the anchor leg.

Everything was happening so fast. She tried to catch her breath.

Coach Wu and Coach Karlsson were shouting things at her from off the course. Mara nodded, but she wasn't really hearing. She knew what she needed to do.

Kirby entered the stadium in third again. Norway was pulling away.

Aggressive. She needed to race aggressively.

Kirby tapped her. A perfect exchange, and Mara's focus zeroed in on Norway. On first place. She easily passed second place again.

Mara pursued Norway, narrowing the lead with every push forward. The big curve on the course was fast and slippery, and Mara had been too conservative on it during the previous legs.

She needed to trust her skis. And herself.

She blew around the curve, gaining on Norway.

They hit the final climb, then the straightaway in the stadium, and she wasn't going to let Kirby down. Using her whole body, every reserve of energy, and every bit of her heart, she closed the gap.

Mara saw Kirby's face, her smile, right before Kirby turned and started skiing, trying to pick up momentum before the exchange. Mara pushed harder to explode through the end of her leg. She let out a yell and tapped Kirby's shoulder.

She got out of the way and put her hands on her knees. Her chest was heaving, and pain was present and accounted for in every part of her body. Even her teeth hurt. She felt ultimately drained. Emotionally and physically.

"Fuck," she gasped, standing up. Tears sprung to her eyes. She was helped out of her skis.

The Norwegian skier she'd been chasing all race gave her a hug, and they both moved to the other side of the finish line to wait for their teammates to complete their last lap.

Mara was still winded when Kirby came into the stadium in second.

She reached the straightaway, and Mara knew how exhausted she'd been by that point. But Kirby didn't look tired. She looked powerful.

She caught Norway. Drew even.

"Come on, Kirby!" Mara screamed.

Kirby had more in the tank, more to give.

One last push, all grit and determination and perseverance, and Kirby passed Norway. She lunged across the finish line. And Mara screamed again. She'd never screamed like that in her life, and she couldn't stop.

Kirby collapsed onto her side, and Mara dove at her.

"You did it! You did it," Mara yelled, grabbing Kirby, wanting to shake her and touch her and hug her. "You did it. Holy shit, Kirby, you did it!"

Kirby grimaced, panting. "*We* did." She loosely wrapped her arms around Mara, and then her arms fell back into the snow like a puppet whose strings had been cut. "I'm tired."

Mara laughed. No shit she was tired.

Mara cupped Kirby's face, cold hands against Kirby's red cheeks. Kirby smiled and sat up.

They had won a gold medal.

Holy shit. They'd won.

And suddenly Mara was sobbing, and she couldn't stop that either.

Kirby pressed her forehead to Mara's, and Mara never wanted to leave that position. In the snow, on their butts, Kirby still strapped into her skis, heads together, and so fucking close.

Kirby shucked off her gloves and gripped Mara's face, skin on skin, her fingertips in Mara's hair. Mara cried harder.

"You finally got your Olympic gold," Kirby whispered.

"*We* did. I didn't want to let you down."

"Never." Kirby wiped a tear away from Mara's cheek with her thumb. "God, Mara."

Then a flag was wrapped around their shoulders. They needed to stand up. They needed to do any number of things, but Mara wasn't moving.

She was soaking up the win with Kirby for as long as she was allowed. For forever if she was allowed.

TWENTY-SEVEN

KIRBY MOVED through the after-race chaos in a daze.

Mara hadn't let go of her hand once. Not when Mara had hugged her parents. Not when Kirby had hugged Apollo, who was lined up to race his team sprint final right after theirs.

It had to have looked suspicious, a bit too friendly, a bit too close, but Kirby didn't care.

And now Mara was talking, talking, talking to the press in the exchange zone like she'd been replaced by a body double.

"You're known for being a stoic competitor, Mara. But you seem quite open and expressive today," Henrik Jensen said. "I've only seen you cry one time, and that was four years ago after losing the thirty-k mass start."

"That day I cried because I was disappointed. Because I'd let myself down, and I was embarrassed. But I didn't race for myself today. I raced *with* my heart. For my heart. For Kirby. And for Brandilyn. I wanted to do my best for them. And I think being vulnerable is why I raced so well. I could let myself *feel* and be aggressive and ski with joy. Because it wasn't about me."

Henrik blinked a few times, clearly surprised by such a wordy answer. "KB, what is it like winning the gold medal with your biggest rival? Much has been made about your rivalry in these last two Olympics."

"I'm… I haven't quite processed it yet. I'm glad we got a chance to write our own chapter in the story, though."

Mara gripped her hand harder, and Kirby squeezed back.

"Mara, you've stated your goal was a gold medal. Does it diminish it that you got gold but it's a team medal, not an individual one?"

"No." Mara's voice cracked, and she started crying again. She really was a puddle. "It's better. Last Olympics, all I could think about was gold, gold, gold, and then we all know what happened. I raced terribly for most of the Games. I started this Olympics the same way. Gold, gold, gold. But today, all that was going through my head was Kirby, Kirby, Kirby. Don't let Kirby down. Close the gap for Kirby. Because I knew she could finish this. And she did. The medal mattered less to me than *her* and the team. And I'll be honest, that has never been the case."

"Okay, princess, save it for your memoir," Kirby said.

And Mara sent her that signature dirty look that Kirby loved so fucking much. Kirby laughed, pulling Mara close into a side hug. Mara leaned into her.

Henrik's eyes went wide.

"Any more questions?" Kirby asked him.

He shook his head. "No. Maybe off the record later. But no. Not now."

Kirby moved them through the after-race press. They did the required drug testing business. Then they reached the changing room to celebrate with the team. Coach Wu was crying. Mara was crying. Apollo, who had come in tenth in his team sprint final, was crying. Even Coach Karlsson was wiping tears away.

But Kirby had never felt less like crying. She felt like shouting. Like letting all the pent up, stored up energy out.

They'd done it. They'd fucking done it, and she had no idea what that meant for her and Mara.

Maybe nothing.

Maybe everything.

Maybe it didn't matter. They'd won a gold medal. She'd done that for Mara. And she believed what Mara had said.

Mara had done it for her too.

Someone crashed into Kirby's back, giving her a huge hug. She turned to find Brandilyn.

Kirby hugged her back. "I'm sorry it wasn't you." And Kirby was. Maybe they wouldn't have won if it had been Brandilyn. But maybe they would have, and she truly was sad for Brandilyn that they would never know.

"Next time."

"Fuck yeah, next time."

"I'm happy it was her," Brandilyn said.

Kirby glanced at Mara, who had finally released Kirby's hand so she could jump up and down with Lindsey.

Kirby was happy it was her too.

She wanted a moment alone with Mara, but who knew when that would happen. Maybe not for hours. For days.

The rest of the afternoon moved around Kirby in bursts. More interviews. More celebrations.

Eventually, they each had a cool hour at the Olympic Village to shower and get ready for the evening medal ceremony, and Mara left her side for the first time.

Once Kirby was under the spray, she started shaking, all the adrenaline leaving her. She laughed and tried to breathe through the ridiculous come down. Racing well was such a high, but she was ready for her heartbeat to calm, for her body to settle.

She needed normalcy, so she took extra minutes in the shower, doing some of the special stuff she didn't always have time for.

She imagined an interviewer asking, *Kirby, what's the first thing you did after winning a gold medal.*

Oh, you know, I took an everything shower—shaved my legs, exfoliated, moisturized my knees and elbows.

She got out of the shower and had finished dressing in her medal ceremony outfit when there was a knock at their door. She heard Jordan answer it.

Kirby peeked out of the bathroom to see who it was, but before she even got eyes on Mara, she knew it would be her.

Mara was making small talk with Jordan, even though Mara sucked at small talk. Her hair was wet, she didn't have makeup on, and she was clearly not fully ready for the medal ceremony, but she'd searched Kirby out anyway.

"Want me to braid your hair?" Kirby asked Mara,

pulling up the first excuse she could think of. "For the medal ceremony?"

"Oh, uh, sure." Mara said.

"Come here."

Mara squeezed into the bathroom with Kirby, and Kirby neatly shut the door.

Then she pinned Mara to it.

"I don't actually want my hair braided for the medal ceremony," Mara said because she was annoying.

"Shut up."

"No."

Kirby tried to kiss her because she felt like she'd vibrate apart if she didn't.

But Mara dodged her. "Wait, KB."

"Fuck." Kirby rested their foreheads together, just like after the race. "Okay."

She had severely misjudged this. And that was the first time Mara had called her KB where it had sounded fond and maybe a little sad instead of mean, and Kirby had no idea what that meant.

"You need to know that I really freaking like you," Mara whispered.

"But?"

"Not because you won me a gold medal."

Kirby laughed. "*We* won." She pulled back and caressed Mara's cheek.

Mara's emotions were right there on the surface, so clear in her bright green eyes. Affection, maybe more than affection. Happiness. Joy.

"I don't know what comes next," Mara said. "But I like you so much. I'm so sorry for saying all that stuff about—"

"Hush."

Mara smiled sweetly, and Kirby was in pieces.

Mara lifted her hand and rubbed a thumb over Kirby's chin, then along her jaw, then up and over Kirby's eyebrow, and for the first time since they'd won, Kirby felt like crying.

"You're beautiful, Kirby," Mara said matter-of-factly as if she'd just noticed.

Then *she* kissed Kirby. A quick press of their lips together. Then a longer one.

Mara stepped away from the door, spun them around so Kirby was against it, and deepened the kiss. She took over. And Kirby melted for her.

A knock on the door they were crushed against made them both jump.

"You guys have to go," Jordan said, and Mara laughed against Kirby's mouth.

Kirby stole one more kiss. "Come on, princess."

TWENTY-EIGHT

"DID you know that the melting point of gold is 1,948 degrees Fahrenheit?" Mara asked as they waited to step onto the top of the podium.

"No, Mara, I did not know that," Kirby said, laughter in her voice.

But Mara did. *Gold, gold, gold.*

Once, it had consumed her.

Kirby's hand was warm in hers. Their names were announced, and they took the big step up onto the top together. They waved at the cheering crowd together.

Together, together, together.

The threat of tears pressed against Mara's chest as she leaned down for the medal to be placed around her neck. After they straightened up, Mara looked at Kirby, who was beaming at her. And those tears welled up and escaped, sliding down Mara's cheeks one after another. There was no stopping them. She didn't even try.

Mara had cried more that day than she had in her entire

life. It felt like she was rewriting everything she'd ever known and believed about emotionality in their sport. She wanted to be vulnerable. For herself. For those watching. And for Kirby. They deserved her true emotions.

And it did feel different, that Olympic gold medal around her neck. Different than the silvers and bronzes.

She smiled at Kirby. She could barely take her eyes off Kirby.

It felt so fucking different.

The national anthem played, and Mara tried to listen. She mouthed the words and watched the flags ripple.

And then it was over.

She lifted the bouquet up and waved it at the crowd.

Kirby hugged her, her hand sneaking to the back of Mara's head and briefly into her hair, which was down and wild and still a little damp.

They released each other to hug the skiers from Norway and Italy. It had been the three teams' race from the beginning, and Mara suddenly felt such an affinity for their competitors, for the strong women who she'd been racing against all over the world for years.

The medal ceremony ended, and they were ushered around, following where handlers pointed them. Mara started to feel a bit lost like she was observing herself float through the experience rather than feeling it.

And, God, she wanted to feel every moment of it. She wanted to enjoy it without worrying about the next race. Or what she'd do in retirement. Or what the heck was going to happen with her and Kirby.

But it was muscle memory for her to be thinking about

the next win. Chasing the next accomplishment. *Goal drift.* And for once, Mara wished she didn't care so much.

"Let's get the fuck out of here," Kirby whispered in her ear.

Mara grabbed Kirby's hand and let Kirby lead her until they were back in the Olympic Village. First to Kirby's room, where Jordan was asleep, then to Mara's room.

Lindsey was gone. She'd left them a note that she wouldn't be back that night. All night.

Such a good teammate.

Kirby dropped the bag of stuff she'd gathered from her room and crowded Mara toward her bed. She gently pushed Mara down onto it and straddled her waist. Kirby touched the gold medal around Mara's neck, running a finger around the edge.

Mara had forgotten she had it on.

"Don't fall into post-success blues," Kirby whispered. "Not yet."

"I don't think I could ever feel blue with you on top of me."

Kirby shot Mara her signature sly grin. "Sweet talker."

"Oh, sure. That's me."

Kirby nodded, unexpectedly serious. "Mara, I like you too. I didn't say that earlier."

Mara tried not to smile. But she failed. Spectacularly.

Kirby liked her.

It was such a silly statement. An obvious statement. But she was overwhelmed by it.

She sat up, forcing Kirby to scoot back and sit in her lap.

Her hands trembled as she took off Kirby's gold medal

and placed it on the bedside table. She unzipped Kirby's jacket, then removed the shirt underneath. And the bra.

Mara looked her fill at Kirby, who was shaking. She was naked from the waist up except for a Team USA beanie. Mara walked her fingertips around Kirby's belly button, over Kirby's ribs, and up to her breasts.

Kirby took in a shuddery breath. She was being rather passive. It was different than the other times they'd done this where Mara had craved being tumbled, being overwhelmed, and Kirby had taken all the control in hand.

This time, Kirby seemed almost thrown and uncertain.

Mara kissed the swell of Kirby's breasts, then the tight tips, and clutched at Kirby's hips, fingertips digging in hard.

"Oh, fuck," Kirby sighed and arched toward her. One of Kirby's hands delved into Mara's hair, knocking her Team USA stocking cap off. The other gripped the ribbon of Mara's gold medal.

Part of Mara wanted to tell Kirby not to wrinkle it. The other part of her recognized it was incredibly hot that she was getting to do this with an Olympic gold medal around her neck.

Mara slid her hands up Kirby's muscled back and took her time painting Kirby's chest and shoulders and neck with kisses.

"God, it's unbelievable how good you feel," Kirby gasped. "Why is it always so good?" She ground against Mara's lap, and Mara knew Kirby would be wet. She would be ready.

"You're just riding high from today," Mara said against Kirby's jaw.

"No." Kirby groaned. "It's you." She leaned back, forcing Mara to stop kissing her neck. "Mara, it's you. *Us.* Can't you see that? It's us."

"Yes." Mara toppled Kirby onto her back. "It's us."

As soon as Kirby was on the bed, she ripped her pants down and off, clearly desperate. Before Mara could react, before she could remove any of her own clothes, Kirby was naked.

Mara climbed on top, pinned her, and kissed her.

"Please, Mara," Kirby whispered against her lips.

Mara bit Kirby's lip, one last sting, and moved down her body. She was starting to feel as frantic as Kirby sounded. As she resettled between Kirby's legs, the gold medal felt too heavy. A nuisance getting in the way.

She yanked it off and tossed it away from them on the bed. She ripped her nice podium jacket off and threw it too.

And then she was on Kirby. Her mouth right where they both wanted it, and Kirby jolted like she'd been shocked.

"Oh God," Kirby said, laughing. "Seeing you fling a gold medal across the room so you can go down on me should not be that hot, but it really fucking is."

Mara didn't have anything to say to that. She didn't have anything to say at all as she licked Kirby's clit, as she filled Kirby with as many rough fingers as she could take.

It's us.

It's us.

Kirby tasted incredible, bright and citrusy. She was

shaking. And being way too fucking loud. And was so amazingly wet against Mara's mouth.

"Mara. Yes. Oh God, *Mara*."

Kirby lifted her hips toward Mara's lips, her tongue, her fingers. And then that tension in Kirby snapped.

It's us.

———

Kirby felt raw and torn open. She was pretty sure she'd shouted Mara's name when she'd come.

So that was cool. And not something people in the neighboring rooms would notice at all.

Mara was still in her fucking podium outfit.

Which Kirby was going to take care of as soon as she could feel her toes.

Even though Mara was mostly dressed, she was not composed. Her eyes were wild, her movements jerky, her hair a complete mess. Her face was wet from Kirby.

And that was very motivating. Kirby sat up and grabbed a fistful of Mara's hair.

Mara's eyes snapped shut immediately, and wasn't that amazing? How easily Mara surrendered.

Kirby leaned forward and licked her taste from Mara's chin and lips.

"Start taking this shit off," she said, tugging on Mara's shirt.

Then she bounded from the bed and grabbed her bag. She unwrapped her favorite toy and rushed back to Mara. Mara had barely gotten her shirt off.

Kirby dragged Mara's pants down, bringing her under-wear with it, but her feet got tangled. They had to struggle and use teamwork to get her naked.

Mara laughed once she was free, and the lightness in that laugh made Kirby's heart stop.

She was so fucking into Mara. Kirby felt so much. A simple laugh, a joyful laugh, made her want to give Mara everything.

"God, I like you," Kirby said. She pinned Mara's legs open roughly and kissed that sweet spot between them.

"Are you talking to me or my…"

Kirby grinned. Mara was too prudish to say the words, to finish the joke, and that was incredibly endearing. "Princess, I was talking to you, but I like your cunt too."

"Don't call me—"

"You love it." Kirby used her tongue to fuck into Mara for several long seconds. Mara shuddered. "Don't lie."

"I'm close."

"Already?" Kirby teased. She liked playing with Mara. She liked skiing with her. And fighting with her. And trash talking with her.

"Shut up. Fuck."

Some of the heaviness in the room had lifted. The weight of what they'd been through, the hurt and bullshit, didn't feel so insurmountable. And their achievement, the gold medal, wasn't important right then either.

Just them. Just their hearts racing. And their laughter. And them.

Mara's body tightened as Kirby swirled her tongue

around her clit, and it hadn't been Kirby's plan to finish her like this, but she was adaptable.

So she let Mara fall apart on her tongue, pleasure rippling through her.

Before Mara had recovered, Kirby put her mouth at Mara's ear.

"Trust me?"

"Yes," Mara said, gasping for breath.

"I'm going to make you come again."

"Umm. I don't normally—"

Kirby ran the tip of the dual stimulation vibrator through Mara's folds, and Mara snapped her mouth shut.

"Yes?" Kirby asked.

"Okay."

Mara was wet. It would be easy to slide right in. And Kirby wanted inside her. She wanted to fuck Mara. In every way possible. With her fingers. Toys. Tongue. Everything.

And she'd get her chance.

She was going to spend as long as Mara let her, as many days, or weeks, or years, chasing that dazed, overcome look in Mara's eyes as Kirby pushed the toy inside and turned it on.

Mara was still breathing hard from her first orgasm when Kirby started fucking her.

"Harder," Mara said, and *that* was Kirby's needy, greedy princess.

Kirby kissed Mara and gave her what she'd asked for. Kirby sucked the soft skin of Mara's tits between her teeth, pulled her hair, held Mara steady. And Mara tried to take control like the little control freak she was.

"Stop," Kirby said after several minutes of Mara meeting the thrusts of the toy with her own. "Turn your brain off."

"Bonham," Mara gritted out, clearly aggravated.

"Oh, back to that, are we?" Kirby laughed. She licked Mara's ear lightly, which sent a shiver through Mara's body, "I want you to imagine the fifty-k."

"What?"

"Yeah." Kirby plunged the toy deep and upped the vibration, leaving it seated. Mara gasped and clutched at Kirby's shoulders. "Imagine what it feels like to hit kilometer forty. When every muscle in your body is burning, and every inhale hurts, and it's all mental."

"*Kirby.*"

"And it's only you. And me. And a fast course. And it comes down to who can suffer the best."

Mara was panting by then, her eyes closed, mouth open. She was still as stone, just taking it. Kirby started fucking her hard again, and Mara submitted in the most beautiful way.

"Sometimes, when you come," Kirby whispered, kissing along Mara's jaw. "*Mmm.* You're close, huh, princess? Sometimes when you come, you look like you do at the end of a race. Breathing hard, chest heaving, body weak, splayed out and collapsing in on yourself."

"Fuck." Mara fisted the sheet underneath her.

They were a mess of sweat and red marks from grasping at each other, from the battle.

Mara opened her eyes, but it was like she couldn't see

Kirby at all, staring right through her. Mara's head rolled on the pillow, and she cried out sharply.

And then she was a quaking, fragile gift in Kirby's arms.

Mara's second orgasm hadn't come easy, but Kirby loved a struggle. She wouldn't have become a cross-country skier otherwise.

TWENTY-NINE

MARA HAD NEVER HAD AS much sex as she had after the team sprint.

At one point, in the middle of the night, after a sleepy round three, Kirby kissed Mara's bicep and asked what they were.

"Are you asking to define the relationship, Kirby?" Mara's arms were heavy. She was so drained.

"I guess so."

Every other time they'd fooled around, they'd fought or miscommunicated or made digs at each other afterward.

Mara wasn't going to let that happen this time.

"We go to Sweden after this," Mara said. The World Cup resumed less than a week after the Olympics ended. "Falun, Lahti, Oslo, Lake Placid," she continued, listing the hosts of the rest of the World Cup events.

"You're so good at schedules," Kirby said, a bit bemused. "Are we gonna fuck our way from Scandinavia to New York?"

Mara's career would be over soon, but her life seemed suddenly open. Like something just as exciting could be starting.

It was hard to say the words. To open herself up to the possibility of hurt. To be vulnerable.

But she'd taken a crash course in vulnerability over the past few days, and nothing but good had come of it.

"How about we date and fuck and fall for each other from Scandinavia to New York?" Mara said.

Kirby rolled on top of Mara, quick as a cat, and framed her face with her hands. "Really?"

"Yeah." Mara shrugged, almost like it wasn't a big deal. But it was a big deal. They both knew it. "What do you have going on in the off-season? Training camps and a TV show?"

"Yes. Probably."

Mara's heart started to race but not in a good way. "Another dating show?" She had no idea how those contractual obligations worked.

"No. It's a game show."

"Like *Hollywood Squares*?"

A slow, affectionate smile spread over Kirby's face. "Kind of. But that reference dates you more than the MySpace one, princess."

"Ugh, stop."

"And what are you going to do this summer?" Kirby asked.

"I have no idea." Most skiers who retired had a plan. They went on to be coaches or motivational speakers or commentators. Mara just wanted to *be*.

"Well, whatever we do, let's do it together," Kirby said.

Mara traced her fingertip over the scar below Kirby's eyebrow. "I'm not doing a game show with you."

"Mara, I say this with all the kindness in my heart, but you don't have enough charisma to be asked on a game show."

A laugh cracked out of Mara. There had never been a truer statement.

"We should sleep," Kirby said.

Mara nodded, her eyes starting to droop at the suggestion.

"Three days and seven hours," she said, drowsiness slurring her words.

"Until?" Kirby brushed fingertips through Mara's hair.

"I win the fifty."

———

The women's mass start fifty kilometer was one of the final events on the last day of the Winter Olympics. Mara and Kirby had been given the television schedule for their dramatic interview with Janette Collins, but by the time the interview and race aired in the US, the Olympics would be over in Italy.

Various moments of trash talk through the years, including the press conference from Beijing, where Mara had truly instigated the animosity and rivalry between them, would also air prior to their race.

They were the big story. Still. Their rivalry. Their history. Trash talk, upsets, trading podiums.

If Mara watched every interview, every contentious interaction, she would be able to track the progression of losing her heart. But she was trying not to think about it. Otherwise, she'd get mushy.

She and Kirby had spent that one blissful night together. They'd woken up early the morning after the team sprint to do more press before turning their focus to the fifty-k. But first, Kirby had marked Mara's body with kisses. She'd left an invisible imprint on Mara to carry with her.

Mara had felt punch drunk. Love drunk. For hours afterward.

They'd hardly spoken since.

Kirby was giving her space to prepare, to rest, to train.

Mara had changed a lot in the past four years. Even more in the past twenty-six days. But she was still *herself*. She needed reflection and focus and alone time.

The morning of the fifty-k was warm. Up over thirty-seven degrees. It would be a slushy slog of endurance. That type of race played to Mara's strengths. She was the best at enduring the misery of a wet, sloppy course.

Mara got ready for the race alone. It was her routine. Lip balm. French braid. Competition sunglasses. The silver ones. They were lucky.

The team and coaches knew to give her a wide berth before a distance race. She needed to mentally prepare as much as physically. And the fifty-k was a mental battle.

Just like Kirby had said.

Mara smiled as she thought about Kirby.

Kirby pushing her to surrender.

Kirby kissing her ear and talking dirty about suffering through her favorite race.

Mara left the changing room, chatted with Coach Karlsson for a few minutes, and joined the huge scrum of racers who would all start at the same time. It would be a melee for position, and Mara intended to be forceful coming off the starting line, to find her footing early, draft with the top of the pack, and run away with it in the end.

Last time, she'd been too confident, and she hadn't left anything in the tank for the finish line. She'd known Kirby had been close, but she'd underestimated her.

This time she was as confident, but she'd never underestimate Kirby—or any other skier—again.

Mara shook out her arms and tuned out the huge din of skiers talking, of bells and yells in the crowd.

They had two minutes before they took their positions on the starting line.

She hadn't seen Kirby once that morning, and suddenly, she knew she wanted to. Needed to.

She glanced around but didn't spot her. They got the signal to begin to line up for the race. Mara's starting placement was toward the front of the throng, her position prime. She moved through the crowd of skiers.

Someone gripped her wrist. She turned to find Kirby smiling at her. Mara stopped and couldn't help but smile back.

Kirby reached up and adjusted Mara's silver sunglasses. It was unnecessary. Mara dressed meticulously, but she liked that Kirby had touched her.

"Break a leg, Mara."

Mara laughed and shook her head.

"Or a pole," Kirby said. "That would be better."

"Don't joke."

"I'm not." Kirby's smile was slow and sexy.

And Mara couldn't help but touch too. She took Kirby's chin between her gloved fingers. Kirby's eyes widened as Mara leaned in and kissed her.

Quick. Perfect. Public.

And then Mara slipped by Kirby to her starting position.

She breathed in the excitement, the thrill in the air. She let the roar of the crowd reach her for once, took it all in.

Then she let it all go. Every thought and worry and preoccupation. All that mattered now was clean technique, stamina, and a fight to the end.

As one, the skiers moved into their starting stances.

This was going to be so freaking fun.

The starting signal popped, and Mara powered off the line and onto the course, her heart exposed, full of joy, and full of grit.

EPILOGUE

Four Months Later

WARM, yellow sunshine filtered through the open blinds and painted stripes over Kirby's sleeping form. Mara traced the streaks of light on Kirby's bare back with her fingers.

Kirby had been exhausted since getting to Alaska two nights before. It was a busy summer off-season for her. She'd been in L.A. for a fast and furious three weeks where she'd filmed a game show, a trivia competition for charity, a few podcasts, two commercials, and interviews and commentary for a mini-docuseries about celebrity villains.

Mara should let her get some rest, but she wasn't feeling particularly generous that morning.

"We need to do a practice run," she whispered in Kirby's ear.

"No."

"Mount Marathon waits for no one."

"Go away." Kirby rolled onto her stomach.

Mara smiled and looked out the window of her camper. The tide was going out in Resurrection Bay, and early risers were out walking their dogs or fishing along the rocky beach. The sun was high. She'd missed the sunrise at 4:40 am, but just barely.

She'd already eaten breakfast, caught up on the news, and gone for a long bike ride through Seward. She was tired of waiting.

"Let's hike to Tonsina Point instead. It's an easy hike," Mara said, hoping a laidback trek would be more enticing than running a difficult five-k with a 3,000-foot elevation gain. They could do their practice run that evening instead.

Four days until the race.

They had plenty of time to figure out their mountain routes.

Kirby turned onto her back, and Mara pounced on her naked body, pinning her down.

"What time is it?" Kirby said, her voice scratchy.

"Six thirty."

"Oh, fuck you, Mara. Leave me alone."

Mara laughed. "No." She kissed Kirby's neck, her shoulders.

"It's too early for this," Kirby said, threading her fingers in Mara's hair and pushing her head lower, completely contradicting her words. "You're supposed to relax during retirement."

Kirby groaned as Mara kissed between her legs.

"I'm relaxed," Mara said.

Kirby arched off the bed as Mara pressed a few fingers inside her. "Slow down."

Mara knew what made Kirby tick. She knew how to finish her faster than it took Kirby to race a sprint. And she wasn't slowing down.

After less than three minutes, Mara sat up and smiled. Kirby was still shaking, her body pulsing around Mara's fingers.

"Let's go do something," Mara said. "I don't want to hang out in the camper all day."

Mara loved her camper. She'd sold her Anchorage condo and bought the trailer as soon as the snow had started to melt. It was small and cozy, full of warm colors and plush cushions and blankets. Perfect for her when she was alone. Even better when Kirby was taking up half the bed.

She didn't know what she would do once winter hit. Probably pay to store it somewhere and follow Kirby to Europe for the World Cup. She was already planning to drive it the whole way to Park City and Vermont as Kirby moved through different summer training camps.

But the Alaska morning was too beautiful to waste another moment inside.

Kirby bodied Mara onto her back like a wrestling takedown.

Okay, maybe Mara could withstand a few more moments inside after all.

"It's too early for this," Kirby repeated, but she followed the words with a kiss. "Damn it, Mara, why are you already dressed to work out?"

Kirby ripped Mara's top off and struggled to remove the bike shorts.

"Because I've already worked out this morning."

Kirby fought to get Mara naked. She didn't help much because Kirby's frustration was funny.

"Hey, did you really say that I only call you *KB* when I'm being nasty? Like did you actually say that in an interview?" Mara said as Kirby tugged the bike shorts off Mara's butt. She'd seen the article that morning—a buzzy, gossipy piece in a fashion magazine. The pictures of Kirby had been incredible.

"Yes. You say *KB* when you're being nasty, *Kirby* when you're being sweet, and *Bonham* when you're pissed at me."

"You're unbelievable. That is too personal. And not true." Except, it kind of was true.

Kirby finally got Mara's shorts off. She flung them to the other side of the camper.

There was a nice, overhead shelf above their bed that Kirby insisted needed to hold their toys. She sat up, grabbed a strap-on, and then she was inside Mara, fucking her hard and fast, in a few seamless movements. They'd had lots of practice at this point.

Mara laughed, joy lifting her to the rafters.

"You'd think," Kirby said between kisses, "that winning a couple Olympic gold medals would satisfy you."

"Is two 'a couple'?"

"Don't critique my grammar right now, Mara May." Kirby gripped a fistful of Mara's hair.

Mara smiled and wrapped her legs around Kirby's waist.

"But you're never satisfied, are you?" Kirby slowed down, switching to long, powerful strokes. She knew what it took to finish Mara fast too. "My greedy little princess. Winning the fifty-k wasn't enough, huh? Or another Crystal Globe. Now you need to bike and hike and run and needle me about pointless interviews. Now you need to win a ridiculous and dangerous race where there will be bears, and we could fall off a cliff."

"We'll be fine." There would be so many people on the mountain during the race a bear sighting would be highly unusual. Mara struggled to get the words out as pleasure started to radiate up her spine and down her legs. "I don't care about winning."

"Bullshit."

"Just want to beat *you*. Again."

Her body detonated, and she moaned through her orgasm. Kirby kissed her softly, gently, peppering her face and neck and shoulders until Mara could breathe again.

"Did the thought of beating me in a race just make you come?" Kirby asked after a few seconds.

Mara laughed again. Laughter came so easily now. She'd never been this happy.

Kirby had learned so much about Mara in the four months since the Olympics had ended.

She'd learned that Mara was as competitive about canasta as she was about racing.

She'd learned that Mara kept all her medals and

trophies in a set of tubs from Costco, which Mara had moved from her own garage to her mom's after she'd sold her condo.

Kirby had met Mara's dad and learned exactly how Mara had ended up so closed off, but she'd also met Mara's mom, who was brilliant and kind and pretty chill about having raised the best cross-country skier in the world.

She'd learned that Mara was terrible at giving interviews about their now public relationship, consistently answering questions about it with the equivalent of a "none of your fucking business." Kirby did the interviews now, which suited them both just fine.

She'd learned Mara was generous, intentional, loving, and honestly such a wonderful girlfriend. If Mara would agree to sleep in until eight occasionally, Kirby would have said she was the best girlfriend ever.

And she'd learned that Mara loved to camp, hike, run, and mountain bike, and took all those endeavors *very* seriously.

"We only have the switchbacks left," Mara said. "Then we'll be at Tonsina Point."

Kirby was dragging on the hike, and Mara's impatience was slipping through.

But Kirby felt like she'd hardly slept in three weeks, she'd been so busy. Plus, she had new anti-anxiety meds on board, and they'd been making her feel groggier than usual. It wasn't a perfect fix, but she was working hard with her doctors to get the right formula of therapy and medicine figured out.

"If you don't want me to be slow, don't wake me up with an orgasm before the sun's even up," Kirby grumbled.

"The sun comes up in the middle of the night here, Bonham. I woke you up mid-morning. Don't be hyperbolic."

Six thirty was not mid-morning.

Kirby grabbed Mara's hand just to touch her. To be closer. They started to make the steep descent down a long series of winding boardwalks.

Large ferns, mossy rocks, and huge trees bordered the trail, like walking through the set of *Jurassic Park*. They finally reached the bottom of the hill and crossed a bridge.

Kirby stopped in her tracks, completely speechless.

In front of them was the most beautiful panoramic ocean view.

"See? Wasn't this worth it?" Mara said. "We could even run back to the trailhead to warm up for—"

"Mara, *shhh*." Kirby dragged her forward by the hand, over the wide expanse of pebbled beach, to get them closer to the sparkling water's edge.

Tall green grass flanked the beach before the landscape climbed back into mountains blanketed by rich, dark forest.

Once Kirby had pulled Mara a couple hundred feet closer to the water, she stopped at a small knoll that was adorned with a huge sun-bleached log. She plopped down in front of the log and leaned back against it. Mara sat beside her.

The log blocked their view of the other hikers who were spending their morning at Tonsina Point as well. It felt like they were the only two people in the world. Just them, the water, and the mountains.

And, God, the mountains. Across the bay, white-tipped peaks seemed to rise out of the ocean like some mythical god had lifted them straight from the sea. Seeing the snowy mountaintops, glaciers, and ice fields made Kirby itch for her skis, even though it was only July. She'd never missed skiing in the summer as much as she did right then. Training and roller skiing wasn't cutting it. She was ready to compete.

She glanced over at Mara. Mara was looking at her, not the tide or the seabirds flying around or the mountains.

Mara's cheeks were rosy from the warmth of the sun and the exertion of the hike. Her hair was in two long French braids, but it was frizzy around her face. She was wearing hiking boots, tall socks, shorts, and a lime green sports bra. She'd pushed her silver sunglasses up onto the top of her head.

She was beautiful. Just as inspiring as the view. Just as sacred to Kirby.

"I love you, Kirby," Mara said.

They'd never said those words to each other, but Mara spoke them as if she said it all the time and it was no big deal.

"Really?"

Mara smiled and rolled her eyes. "No, I'm lying."

She looked back at the water like that was that. Like she didn't give a shit what Kirby might say back. Like she was secure in the knowledge that speaking those words into existence was enough.

"Are you saying that because you feel bad about the torture you're going to put me through running Mount Marathon?" Kirby said.

"You're a world-class athlete. An Olympian who recently won a medal in every event you competed in. Running up a little hill will be no big deal."

Mount Marathon, a mountain on the outskirts of Seward, was not a little fucking hill. The race was considered the toughest five-k on the planet. In a few days' time, they would try to conquer it. It was over three miles total, almost 3,000 feet of elevation gain in less than one mile, and averaged a thirty-four-degree incline with a sixty-degree incline at its steepest. It wasn't so much a run as a vertical climb. And then they had to run down. Which wasn't so much a run as a fall. Kirby's goal was to be conservative and not break a leg.

Mara's goal was to follow the tradition of the many cross-country skiers who had won.

"Mara May," Kirby said, her voice shaky.

"Hmm?"

Kirby turned Mara's face back toward her. Mara's lips were tipped up into a knowing smile.

"I love you too."

One of Mara's eyebrows went up for half a second, and her smile transformed from knowing to joyous. "You sure?"

"Yeah. I'm sure."

Mara nodded and rested her forehead against Kirby's just like after their team sprint gold medal.

"I'm going to smoke you on Saturday," Mara murmured.

"You'll be so far ahead of me, I won't even see the smoke, princess."

Mara pulled back and stared at Kirby for a long, intense moment, and Kirby realized she'd unintentionally repeated a bastardization of that very first potshot Mara had ever taken at her. Way back during the Beijing Olympics. Over four years ago.

I don't see Kirby Bonham as a rival. I'm usually so far ahead of her, I don't see her at all.

The beginning. The best thing that had ever happened to Kirby. Without that trash talk, they would never have fought and fallen in love.

"I knew then," Kirby said. "Thinking back on it."

A salty breeze ruffled their hair, and Mara cupped Kirby's cheek, her eyes sparkling with emotion.

"Knew what?" Mara asked.

"That we were meant to live this life together in one way or another. As competitors. Rivals. Lovers. We belonged side-by-side."

Tears welled and slipped down Mara's cheeks. With no warning, she kissed Kirby soundly.

Then Mara jumped to her feet, kicked off her hiking boots, pulled off her socks, and looked down at Kirby sitting in the sand.

She grinned and roughly wiped her tears away. "Race ya."

"Where to?"

Mara shrugged. "Wherever you want to go." Then she took off, running toward the water lapping gently at the shore.

And Kirby followed.

LOVE ON THE PODIUM

**Don't forget to check out the other queer sports romances in the
Love on the Podium series.**

————

Ski-Crossed Lovers by Allison Temple

A Good Puck by Rochelle Wolf

On The Button by Jaime Samms

A Gold Medal in Love by Alex La Bruyere

AUTHOR'S NOTE

FREE BONUS SCENE

I hope you enjoyed *Cross-Country Love* as much as I loved writing it. If you'd like to see where Kirby and Mara are eight years after the Milan Cortina Olympics, check out a bonus scene available to my **newsletter subscribers**. It is written in the style of a celebrity profile or magazine feature.

YOUR NEXT READ

If you liked *Cross-Country Love*, you might also like **Party Favors**, which is a super sexy, online-friends-to-lovers, sapphic romance novella set over New Year's Eve. It has hot girls, hot toys, and hot lingerie.

ACKNOWLEDGMENTS

A huge thank you to the other authors in the Love on the Podium series: Allison, Rochelle, Jaime, and Alex. It's been so fun doing this with you.

Endless gratitude to Susie Selva for great editing, Jenn Burke for eagle-eyed proofreading, and Jo Clement for an awesome cover design. I'm very thankful to have you all on my team.

To the athletes who answered my questions, even when you didn't know why I was asking—you are all an inspiration. Special thanks to Kate and Sara. And *extra* special thanks to Neva for helping me connect with the web of elite winter athletes in Alaska.

Hugs to Karen Kiely and Neva Post (again) for the writing dates and the beta reading. I wouldn't have written this book without you. And to Allison Temple and Layla Reyne for keeping me inspired and motivated. You're all the best writing friends I could ever ask for.

And lastly, all the love to my husband for holding down the (often literal blanket) fort.

ALSO BY ERIN MCLELLAN

So Over the Holidays Series

Stocking Stuffers

Candy Hearts

Bottle Rocket

Party Favors

Spring Breakup

Bold Brew Universe

Perfect Matcha

Farm College Series

Controlled Burn

Clean Break

Love Life Series

Life on Pause

Life of Bliss

Storm Chasers Series

Natural Disaster

Small City Heart

"What Happens in Tulsa"

ABOUT THE AUTHOR

Erin McLellan writes queer contemporary and erotic romance. She lives in Alaska with her family. She is a lover of chocolate, camping, hiking, antiquing, gardening, Dr Pepper, and reality TV.